THE UNEXPECTED LIFE OF
OLIVER CROMWELL PITTS

Also by Avi

The UNEXPECTED LIFE *of* OLIVER CROMWELL PITTS

Being an Absolutely Accurate Autobiographical Account of My Follies, Fortunes & Fate

Written by Himself

AVI

Algonquin Young Readers   2017

Published by
Algonquin Young Readers
an imprint of Algonquin Books of Chapel Hill
Post Office Box 2225
Chapel Hill, North Carolina 27515-2225

a division of
Workman Publishing
225 Varick Street
New York, New York 10014

LIBRARY OF CONGRESS CATALOGING-IN-PUBLICATION DATA
Names: Avi, [date] author.
Title: The unexpected life of Oliver Cromwell Pitts / Avi.
Description: First edition. | Chapel Hill, North Carolina : Algonquin
Young Readers, 2017. | Summary: In 1724 England, twelve-year-old Oliver
Cromwell Pitts embarks on a journey from his seaside home in Melcombe
Regis to London to find his father and his older sister, a journey filled
with thieves, adventurers, and treachery.
Identifiers: LCCN 2016042923 | ISBN 9781616205645
Subjects: | CYAC: Runaways—Fiction. | Criminals—Fiction. | Voyages
and travels—Fiction. | Great Britain—History—George I, 1714–1727—
Fiction. | LCGFT: Historical fiction.
Classification: LCC PZ7.A953 Un 2017 | DDC [Fic]—dc23
LC record available at https://lccn.loc.gov/2016042923

10 9 8 7 6 5 4 3 2 1

First Edition

For Amanda, Cindy, Tom, and Willy

England, 1724

CHAPTER ONE

In Which I Introduce Myself after Which I Immediately Plunge into a Desperate Situation.

On November 12, 1724, I, Oliver Cromwell Pitts, lay asleep in my small room at the top of our three-story house, when, at about six in the morning, I was shocked into full wakefulness by horrible sounds: roaring, wailing, and screeching.

Confounded by such forceful clamors, I was too frightened to shift from my bed. Even so, I listened hard, trying to make sense of what was occurring. It did not help that the room in which I lay had no windows, so I could see little. Then I realized that my bed—in fact, our entire house, an old wooden structure—was shaking. The combination of darkness and dreadful sounds made everything worse.

I dared not move, in hopes that by remaining still, I

might diminish both noise and quivering. Yet as if to mock me, the uproar only grew louder and more frenzied, rising to a horrifying crescendo.

Desperately wanting to see something, the better to gain intelligence as to what was occurring, I reached toward the floor where I had placed my candle and flint box the night before, only to discover they were not there. The shaking of the house was so forceful it must have tumbled them away. The next moment I heard a slapdash thumping directly overhead, as if stones were hitting our thatched roof.

Midst all this confusion, I recognized the boom of crashing waves. Even this familiar sound was no comfort: My family home in the English town of Melcombe Regis was a tenth of a mile from the sea. I should not be hearing such near water. I had to investigate.

I crept from bed, fumbled for my clothing, and despite the darkness, dressed swiftly. As I was pulling on my boots, a ghastly splintering sound erupted directly overhead. I looked up. To my astonishment, a faint light appeared as a piece of our roof peeled away like a strip of orange rind, leaving a large and jagged hole. In an instant, a torrent of frigid water poured down, drenching me. What's more, the wailing sounds grew louder, which I now identified as wind.

Tempests often struck the Dorset coast, but in all my

twelve years I had never experienced one so violent. The storm must have hit the shore at high tide—under a full moon—a linking of meteorological conditions, which now and again brought flood. I truly wondered if the world was coming to an end. And if not the entire world, surely my world seemed to be collapsing fast.

Little did I know how accurate that notion would come to pass.

At that immediate moment, however, my concern was this: I must warn my sister of the danger. Charity—for that was my beloved sister's name—had her room below mine. Yet no sooner did I think of cautioning her, than I remembered she—six years older than I—had thankfully gone to London two months ago to live with our uncle Tobias Cuttlewaith.

Good, I thought. She, at least, was safe.

It was only natural then that my worries turned next to my father, Mr. Gabriel Pitts—to give his whole name. A lawyer, he had his closet—which is to say his office and private room—on the first level of our house.

Wanting to make sure he was safe, I floundered about in search of the stairs. Ineptly, I found them, and then descended with great caution through the blustery, sodden darkness. The water, coming through the torn roof, was flooding the stairway, making it slippery.

After a brief descent, during which I guessed rather

than saw my location, I reached the second level, where my sister had her room. It was a little brighter than my chamber, but such powerful gusts were whipping about that I became convinced a wind had smashed the lone window in.

"Father!" I cried, but the sounds that roared about me were louder than my voice. To find him I would have to go down another flight of narrow steps. Accordingly, I gripped the banister as tightly as I could. Halfway down I began to hear sloshing sounds. That suggested that the sea was nearer than I previously thought.

"Father!" I cried again, but received no more reply than before.

Where could he be? Was he hurt? Had he drowned? Could I save him?

As close to panic as I have ever felt, I picked my way down almost to the bottom step where I perceived shimmering liquid pooling below me. Clinging to the wet banister, wondering how deep the water was, I suddenly felt a gob of water on the back of my neck. It so startled me, my fingers slipped, and I plunged headfirst into the water.

In short, I was in grave danger of drowning right in the middle of my own home.

CHAPTER TWO

I Provide Some Vital Information about My Family.

No doubt it is unkind of me—the obligatory author of my autobiography—to leave myself—and you—in such a precarious predicament, possibly drowning and thus in danger of ending my life and my tale too hastily. But before I go forward, you need to learn something about the life I lived.

I shall begin, therefore, at my beginning.

My parents lived in an old three-story wooden house along the short alleyway known as Church Passage near the corner of St. Mary Street in the ancient English town of Melcombe Regis.

Melcombe Regis exists in Dorset County, on the southern coast of England. It is linked to a sister town,

Weymouth, by a sixty-yard-long drawbridge over the Wey River.

Mr. Daniel Defoe (the man who authored *The Life and Strange Surprising Adventures of Robinson Crusoe*) wrote that Melcombe was a "sweet, clean and agreeable town. . . . 'Tis well built, and has a great many substantial merchants in it, who drive a considerable trade and have a good number of ships belonging to the town."

The two towns, Melcombe Regis and Weymouth, share a small, busy harbor, its ships trading with France, Spain, and the American colonies. Being an international seaport, it has endless legal complications requiring resolution: custom duties, taxes, foreign ships, rowdy seamen, and smuggling. Furthermore, ships, both English and foreign, are often tossed upon the stormy Dorset shore and wrecked, which created more legal difficulties. These legal entanglements—and the fees attached—attracted my lawyer father to move from London. Over time he would earn an income between fifty and sixty pounds per year, providing a comfortable life.

His wife, my mother, Hannah Cuttlewaith, left her family in London to come with him. Let it be known—for it is a key to understand what transpired—that my father refused her dowry, denouncing marriage settlements as a barbarous practice meant for the buying and selling of wives.

Consult the Melcombe parish birth records and you will discover that my sister, Charity, was born in 1706, I in 1712, both during the reign of Good Queen Anne.

Alas, I have the unhappy task of informing you that shortly after my mother gave birth to me, she died, an all-too-tragic occurrence of our times.

My father's great shock and distress at the death of my mother, a woman he much loved, made him bitter, angry, and joyless, and filled him with the belief that the world had no sympathy for sorrow. "People care nothing for suffering," he said to Charity and me so often it became a family motto. "To get on you must mask your heart with false smiles."

Let it be said in these early pages that my father, a deeply unhappy man, never smiled. So it was that he named me after Oliver Cromwell, the unflinching Puritan from the previous century, whom my father admired for beheading a king and then becoming the ironfisted Lord Protector of England.

In matters of religion Father became a Nonconformist and in politics, an anti-monarchy man, holding resolutely that "The law is king," a phrase he expressed to all people on all occasions whether relevant or not. He was ill-shaved, poorly dressed, and wore a dirty neckcloth and an ill-powdered wig. Big and heavy, he was reluctant to move in body or mind and thus came to be considered a clumsy, discordful, meddlesome man. All in all he was self-neglected, just as he neglected his children.

Although I chose to believe my father was fond of my sister and me, his ongoing belligerent melancholy was such that he preferred to spend his days with clients, men accused of crimes by wealthy tradesmen or Crown magistrates. As a result, my father had many enemies among the town's establishment. This gave rise to another favorite saying: "A man should be known, not by his friends but by his enemies." And known he was, for he had many a foe in both towns, his reputation being that of a radical, interfering hot-mouth.

Being a lawyer, Father constantly warned my sister and me not to become entangled in the law because of its extreme severity. To steal anything worth even a few shillings was punishable by death or transportation. I cannot tell you how often he told us about the nine-year-old London boy who broke a window to steal twopence worth of paint and hanged for that ghastly crime.

Father never got over the death of my mother and did not remarry. Instead, my father informed Charity—a child only six years old—that she must take care of me and our home. "I will have no servants," he declared. "It demeans both master and servant.

"To be sure," he informed my sister, "I will provide

you with a house and a weekly allowance so you may feed us. The rest is your responsibility."

Father spent his days working, while most nights he went off to an inn. Upon staggering home he often did a singular thing: He would dissolve into syrupy tears and to my sister and me announce, "I have not been a good parent. I promise to do better."

Beware the sinner who continually repents; the more he repents, the greater his need for repentance. So it was Father often repented. He did not change.

Nonetheless, Charity did what my father asked of her—took care of the household. In contrast to him she often shared many a smile. She was prudent and cheerful; she cleaned with care and cooked. She kept our house and me neat as needles. She did it so well she was called "little mother" by nearby neighbors and by town folk in general. It was meant as a compliment. Indeed, the sweet, loving, and pretty girl that Charity was gave up her normal child-hood to be mother to me.

I loved Charity deeply. I turned to her—not Father—when in need of anything, be it food, comfort, or advice, or any of the forms of love a mother provides.

As to my appearance, which readers seem to want to know so as to gain a better sense of a book's hero—whom I humbly believe is me—my curly brown hair was more often than not an unruly mop, which gave an impish quality to my generally merry face—or so my sister claimed. Despite my powerful namesake, I was a small, delicate child. Even as I grew older, people thought me younger than my true age so that they would consider me inept while my constant cheerfulness was taken as simplicity. My diminutive stature, winsome, polite habits, and willing smiles generally induced people to have a protective attitude toward me. Those that didn't protect me bullied me.

Let it be said that I grew up well enough, content with my life in Melcombe. I went to the St. Thomas Street Free School for Boys until I was eleven. I learned to read and write and gained some skill with numbers. I played with other boys along the fine, sandy bayside beaches or in the old fort at the Narrows.

We boys also liked to linger by the river docks, watching ships unload their cargoes while observing the intricate tar-coated rigging, the ropes and gear of seafaring work. I was particularly taken by the sailors who traveled to the American colonies, Chesapeake Bay, in my mind, being a most glamorous place. We wanted to be sailors, or as we boys called them, water-dogs.

When I turned eleven my regular schooling came to an end. Father made me his apprentice so that I might follow him into the legal profession. I spent my mornings studying legal books, though I understood very little of them. Afternoons I would follow my father about when he met with clients or stood before magistrates. While I found it boring, my familiarity of the law—which will be mentioned on these pages—came about by attending Father when he practiced his profession.

But then, in the early fall of 1724, when I was twelve years of age, Charity made a shocking announcement.

CHAPTER THREE

In Which I Tell You What Charity Did.

The day after her eighteenth birthday, Charity announced to Father that she wanted more in her life than to be a "little mother" to her younger brother in a small seaside town.

"But what would you do?" said my father, altogether aghast.

"I intend to go to London," she said.

"London!" cried my father. "London is the most monstrous of cities. Half a million in population. Full of riches, yes, but fuller yet of poverty, corruption, and crime. A place where public hangings are popular entertainment. How could you, an eighteen-year-old girl, go there alone?"

"I won't be alone," returned Charity. "I wrote to my mother's brother, Mr. Tobias Cuttlewaith. Our uncle replied to say that he and his wife would welcome me into his home—as near relatives should—and provide me with protection and employment. He has a well-established gentleman's business."

"You wrote to him?" cried my father. "And he wrote back? Why did I never see these letters?"

"I offered them, but you were too engaged with your enemies and told me to leave you alone."

"Humph. May I remind you I have the legal right to prevent you from leaving. And the law is king."

"Father," replied my sister, "I've spent my youth taking care of you and Oliver. While I love you both, I've had little of my own youth. I wish to see and experience more of the world before I become older. As you say, London is a city of half a million. Melcombe has but four thousand souls."

"You mean you wish to find a husband," said my father with unashamed anger. "Marriage only leads to sorrow."

"That's your experience," Charity returned with a saucy smile, which, as I looked on, surprised me much. "You," she said to Father, "are so disliked in both towns, and have made so many enemies, I'm not likely to find an attractive suitor here. If anyone did ask for my hand in marriage, you most likely would chase him away."

"What about your brother?" my father asked.

"He's old enough to care for himself."

The more my sister spoke, the more astonished I

became. But then, is anything more startling than to observe your sister or brother—your playmate—suddenly turn into an adult?

"London is very far away," my father protested.

"It's but one hundred and twenty-eight miles."

"How do you know that?"

"I inquired. In any case, I intend to take the stagecoach."

"That will cost a whole pound."

"I have saved money from the allowance you have given me."

Father frowned. "All I can say is that if you go, it shall mean hard times for me and your brother."

"The world cares nothing for suffering," Charity reminded him. "To get on you must mask your heart with false smiles."

I smiled, although my father did not.

Father frowned and said, "You are right. I have not . . . been a good parent. I promise to do better."

"I have heard that many times before. I am going," said Charity.

"Let me see the letter from your uncle," he demanded. "It has been years since I knew the man. He was an untrustworthy rascal then. I doubt he has improved."

"Father, you are suspicious of everyone," said Charity, and she handed him our uncle's letter and left the room.

I followed her out. Catching her by her apron strings, I said, "Are you really leaving?"

Charity knelt down upon the floor—she was much taller than I—put her hands on my shoulders, and looked lovingly into my face.

"Oliver, I have not regretted spending most of my life taking care of you. But I must do something for myself before I become a spinster, without any joys of my own.

"I shall say nothing against Melcombe or Weymouth," she continued. "They are fine places. But London, I'm sure, is far more exciting."

"But Father won't be able—"

She cut me off. "Don't you think I have the right to some pleasures?"

What could I say? Ashamed of my selfishness, I gave her my cheerful face and nodded.

"Then will you give me your blessing?"

Though my heart was breaking, I put my arms around her, and with a smile said, "Of course I will! Only send for me when you can."

"Absolutely!" she returned. "Uncle Cuttlewaith has promised me all the comforts of home. For the moment you'll need to take care of Father. I fear he can't do for himself. Besides his drinking, gambling, and bad moods, he argues with everyone. I need to get beyond that. When

I am completely settled, you have my word, you shall join me."

"What if Father doesn't give you permission?"

"It doesn't matter; I've managed to find the money to take me there."

"Was it truly from your household allowance?" I asked, deeply impressed.

She put a finger to my lips. "You needn't know from where it came. Just know I am determined."

As it happened, Charity did not have to pay from her own funds. Albeit reluctantly, Father gave permission and money. His sole caution was that if he discovered that she fell into any kind of hazard, he would immediately bring her home, by legal force if necessary.

He wrote a letter to Uncle Cuttlewaith. A letter was returned, arrangements went forward.

So it was that early one morning, Father, Charity, and I walked to the Bear Inn, the starting point for the London stagecoach.

As I carried her small bag of belongings, I was mazed how lady-like she looked in a long dark blue-and-white dress, gauze apron, stiff bodice, and kerchief over her long chestnut hair. She was, as always, ungaudy and neat, with not a hair out of place.

"Coach to London, please," she said to Mr. Webber, the innkeeper and seller of stagecoach tickets.

To which Mr. Webber replied, "Twenty shillings in the coach. Fifteen shillings on the roof. Ten shillings in the basket."

My sister counted out one pound in silver coins— twenty shillings. My father, frowning, added more money for food and lodging along the way. Then we helped her take an inside seat on what was called the flying coach. Once there she tucked her feet into the straw heaped on the floor, so as to keep her feet warm. We bid her a safe journey with many a "Good-bye" and "Be safe," and my father's final words, "Live straight and true with all the morality I have taught you."

My sister gave me a smiling wink while I gave her a kiss and then she was gone. I thus lost not just my sister, but the one who had been a mother to me.

As Father and I walked home, I was quite down-hearted. "Does it take the coach long to reach London?" I asked.

"Five days," he said, oblivious to my grief.

"That fast!" I said, thinking how quickly she was going from me.

"It is not called a flying coach for nothing. It goes as quickly as possible by changing horses at the inns along the way."

That is how my sister went, leaving me to take care of myself and Father. Once she was gone I was given a small allowance for food, which was to be spent for Father and myself. But, let it be said, once she left, taking her order and cleanliness with her, our household slipped into shambles.

I waited for Charity's summons to join her in London. It did not come. I was sure she had forgotten me. Then, three months after she departed, the terrible storm struck Melcombe Regis and I found myself facing death by drowning in the parlor of our home.

CHAPTER FOUR

In Which I Let You Know if I Drowned.

Though it was a severe shock for me to plunge into the ocean right in the middle of my own home, it was a relief to realize that the cold water was not deep. Thrashing and splashing, I managed to get on my feet and stand in what amounted to twenty-four inches of seawater, up about my knees. Of course, I was dripping wet, shivering with cold, and could do naught but look about with dismay.

Despite the mungy light, I saw that our two front windows had been blown in and the entire room water-soaked. Chairs were overturned. My father's much-prized standing clock had tumbled, its lead pendulum flung out like a broken heart. The fireplace was drenched, its brick hearth muddy. Dishes and pots were scattered and shattered. The paint on the walls had begun to lift like damp bark from an old tree. Even as I stood there, Father's white porcelain teacup floated by.

As I tried to make sense of the chaos, the storm began to abate. Dark skies eased. A streak of sunlight began to illuminate the house. It had been a ferocious but quick tempest.

Then I realized there was a tiny light coming from the stub of a burning candle in a smoky glass lantern on the mantel over our hearth. The glass must have kept the flame from blowing out.

Seeing it reassured me, for surely where there was a burning candle, there would be a person nearby, which is to say, my father.

When I took up the lantern I noticed a piece of paper lying beneath it, as if the lamp with its lit candle was there to call attention to it. Alas, though the paper was covered by writing, many of the letters were smudged by water. Too impatient and agitated to decipher the spoiled words, I left the paper where I found it, and with the lantern continued to search for Father.

I splashed through water to his room at the back of the house and held up the lantern. The room was deserted, although Father's high, heavy desk remained where it was normally placed. The stool upon which he usually sat had been toppled. His high bed, built against the far wall, was empty, its bedclothes rumpled. Everything was thoroughly waterlogged. Even his beloved legal volumes, on their tall shelves, were wet. As for the floor, it was awash with floating papers, the ink floating off the pages like blue-black clouds.

Midst the flotsam of papers and writing quills, a few small, leather-bound books bobbed about. Also, my father's chamber pot. An upright bottle of ink floated by like a little black tub. The bowl of sand used to blot his writing had no doubt sunk.

Then I noticed that Father's wig was not hanging on its accustomed wall peg. He wore that wig whenever he left the house. To be sure, it was not usually freshly powdered or perfumed, but a gentleman to go abroad without his wig—he would say—was not done. Unless it was afloat somewhere about the house—and I had yet to see it—its absence suggested he had taken it with him.

I stepped out through the narrow rear door, into the fenced-in yard that contained our privy.

He was not there.

It occurred to me that he could have retreated upstairs to the safety of my sister's room where I had not investigated. In haste, lantern in hand, I climbed back to the second floor only to learn he was not there either. Even as I began to realize I was quite alone in the house—and perhaps in the world—the lantern candlelight faded away.

I am sure you will be sympathetic when I say that

I—a twelve-year-old boy—was not at all sure what to do. I did recall my father's oft given advice about masking your heart with false smiles. But to think of such advice at such a moment brought tears, not smiles.

As it happened, I was standing in my sister's room where she had affixed a small looking glass to the wall. Trying to act upon Father's advice, I stood before it and manufactured a cheerful smile. It was not powerful, but it was a smile and my smile is truly winsome. I should acknowledge I was rather braced and energized by following his advice. It was a lesson I intended to follow.

I made my way back down the steps, making sure I did not slip. Once below, I stepped again into the first-floor water, which had begun to ebb. As soon as I opened the front door, the remaining water began to sluice from the house. I went out, too.

Though the wind still bore some bluster, the rain was slight while the sky held only scudding gray clouds and some rosy light in the east.

Our forecourt was muddy, with puddles everywhere, making it hard to see the cobblestones. A heap of bricks lay there, too. I stared at it for a few moments before realizing it was the remnants of our fallen chimney.

I glanced up toward the top of neighboring houses, built close to one another. They were mostly wooden, but some were made of the local portland stone. Any number of chimneys had been blown down and thatched roofs had been shredded. Roof tiles on some of the finer stone houses had ripped away and were scattered on the street. Here and there, even the lead sheeting used to waterproof roofs had rolled up, scroll-like. One building had no roof at all.

As I stood wet and shivering at the sight of the damaged, broken houses, Mr. Tickmorton, our next-door neighbor, emerged from his house. He was dressed in his linen nightshirt and nightcap, his feet bare.

An elderly man, he lived alone. Rather stooped and shriveled, he was bald and toothless, which made him look like an aged baby. Much of his conversation was a mumble, but to compensate he spoke loudly.

"Mr. Tickmorton, sir," I called. "Have you seen my father?"

The old man turned slowly, revealing a face that showed confusion and dismay, perhaps a mirror image of my own. Despite the fact that I was someone he saw every day, he gazed upon me as if he had no idea who I was. Worse, without saying a word, he stumbled back into his own house.

Clearly, Mr. Tickmorton was in such a state of storm-shock that I could expect little help from him. It made me wonder if the whole town would be the same.

CHAPTER FIVE

In Which I Search for My Father and Make a Huge Discovery.

I walked down St. Mary's Street where cobblestones were littered with debris: pieces of wood, bricks, wet books, branches, and broken window frames. Even a bed. People were flinging ruined objects out of doors and windows. Others were piling broken and sodden furnishings by their front doors. Overheard conversations were entirely devoted to the fast-moving storm and its devastation.

I greeted people with my best smile and inquired as to their health. I cannot say I was given equal comfort, but rather received scowls and mutterings, as if my cheerful face offended them. Nonetheless, I managed to ask some people if they had seen my father.

"Mr. Pitts? Has he wandered off again? Asleep on some back street. Some inn?"

"I don't know what happened to him," I said. "He's vanished."

One man, upon overhearing this remark, muttered, "A good riddance."

I made no reply to such unkindness.

Struggling to keep the smile on my face, I hurried on, hoping I might see friends. None appeared.

I soon reached the customs house, a three-story brick building, with an elegant stone entrance. Standing by the river Wey and the docks, it was not far from the new bridge to Weymouth.

The river tide was unusually low, exposing the sandy bottom. The docks, where ships were usually tied, were quite deserted. Only when I looked toward the Back Bay—situated behind town—did I see some boats, presumably there for safety. That suggested there had been advance warning about the oncoming storm. Seaside people have ways of predicting weather. Though I had not heard those warnings, I wondered if Father had. Perhaps he took refuge somewhere.

The customs house doors being locked, it was obvious my father was not there. I continued to wander about town, asking anyone and everyone if they had seen my father. No one had. Worse, no one seemed to care. I knew he had been disliked; now I learned how deep that hostility was.

I inquired at the Crown and Scepter, the tavern my father frequented during the day. No one had seen him.

I went on to the Golden Lion Inn, the establishment where my father played nightly games of backgammon. The only one about the inn was the cook, a Mrs. Grady.

Mrs. Grady was a short squab of a woman, who had always been kind to me and my sister when we guided Father home, at such times that he was unable to navigate the passage on his own.

She immediately asked me about the damage to our house.

"The first floor was flooded with water," I told her.

"Is it livable?"

"I don't know. Please, madam, have you any idea where my father might be?"

"He was here last night, early eve. As usual, he won a lot of money at his game with Mr. Bartholomew. The customs master lost so much he stomped away in a frothing anger.

"Soon after, I noticed that a letter . . . no, two letters . . . were delivered to your father. Your father read them. At least one of them seemed to upset him because he left in haste. Was it due to the letters or the storm? I can't say."

She patted my shoulder, and I returned her kindness with a smile.

"Yes, be cheerful. There are some, I've heard, that drowned in the suddenly rising waters."

"I haven't found Father's body," I said, as if that was a hopeful statement. All the same, I had to wonder what those two letters had been, if they had something to do with his disappearance.

"Have you had your breakfast?" Mrs. Grady was kind enough to ask.

I shook my head.

"Well now, you just sit down by my fire, get warm, dry yourself, and I'll bring some food."

I thanked the woman and sat, glad for the drying warmth inside and out. Even when I had eaten all she offered—hot milk, blue cheese, and bread—I remained thinking about those letters my father had received.

Mistress Grady came back to me and said, "I know your 'little mother' has gone to London. Can you tell her what's happened?"

"Please, madam, I'm afraid I don't know where she is."

Her eyes filled with concern. "Have you some money?"

"Not really," I admitted.

"Then, Master Oliver, I fear you've become a homeless, moneyless child. You'll need to report to the town magistrates. Your father being a lawyer, I'm sure you understand something of the law."

My father's phrase, the law is king, went through my head.

"Besides," she continued, "they might have some news about your father. Or help you find him. How old are you?"

"Twelve."

"Are you? You look younger."

"Ask Mr. Buffin at the Free School; he'll tell you."

Paying no mind to what I said, Mrs. Grady said, "If you are under eleven you will be delivered to the children's poorhouse."

"The poorhouse?" I cried.

I had heard many awful stories about those who were sent to the poorhouse. Friends reported that when they misbehaved they were threatened with the place. If my sister and I complained about my father's long hours of work or neglect, he would retort, "I am trying to keep you out of the children's poorhouse. It is no better than Newgate Prison."

So you may be certain it was the last place I wished to go.

"Why, sure," said Mrs. Grady, no doubt seeing consternation on my face, "if your father has perished, your mother already passed, and your sister gone to London you don't know where, you'll be considered an orphan. And if you are an orphan, you'll be grateful for the poorhouse, which will take care of you with kindness."

Alarmed by such a prospect, I immediately got up, thanked the woman for breakfast, gave a smile, and hurriedly left the Golden Lion Inn.

Melcombe had one other inn, the Bear, the place from which the stagecoach left for London, the one Charity had taken. It was on the edge of town, and thereby not a place my father frequented with any regularity. Wanting to check everywhere, I looked there, too.

I asked for Mr. Webber, the Bear's innkeeper, only to be informed—by his stable-boy—that Mr. Webber had gone into town to deal with damaged property. "Have you seen Mr. Pitts, my father?" I asked.

"Lawyer Pitts?" was the reply. "He took the early morning stage to London right before the storm. All in a hurry, he was. As was the stage driver. Suppose he got word of the coming weather. Hope Mr. Pitts reached London safely." He grinned. "Lots of reports coming in about highwaymen robbing and killing. But don't worry," he added, clearly enjoying that he had upset me. "The driver keeps a blunderbuss or a brace of pistols with him."

CHAPTER SIX

In Which I Learn Some More Significant Things.

I was much shaken: In the early morning, just before the storm, my father had gone to London. In an instant, my head was full of questions.

Why had he not told me he was going?

Why didn't he take me with him?

When would he be coming back?

His actions were unlike anything he had ever done before. I had no memory of his ever going to London. Nonetheless I refused to believe my father had abandoned me. I kept telling myself he must have had important reasons.

I had some clues: Just before going, he had received two letters, one of which—according to Mrs. Grady—upset him. Furthermore, the stable-boy had said he was in a hurry. Did Father leave abruptly so as to avoid the storm?

You may be equally sure that I, learning about his departure, spent considerable time wondering when he would return. He had told me that it would take Charity five days to get to London. Presumably it would take another five days to come back. Assuming he went there on business, which would take some time to conclude, if I calculated properly he could well be gone for fifteen days!

Though not knowing when he would return or even where he went, I told myself I must stay in the house—though wet, distressed, and cold—until he returned.

And yet with the chimney down, what would I do for warmth? It was the month of November. True cold was drawing near. There would be frosts soon. I was not sure I had any food. The next question was of crucial importance as it was logical: Was there any money in the house?

The more I pondered these problems, the more distressed I grew. How would I manage? Oh, how I wished my sister, Charity, was about! She would have known what to do.

I plodded back to our house, thinking on Mrs. Grady's words; if I were deemed an orphan, I would be taken up by the town magistrates and put into the children's poorhouse. Already regretting I had told her of my situation, fearful of what might happen if she did tell anyone else, I was reluctant to share my circumstances with others. I also considered going to the Free School and asking Mr. Buffin to write a testimony as to my true age, but before I could make up my mind to do so I arrived home.

What I found was that although the seawater had drained away, a few shallow puddles remained on the first floor. There was mud everywhere as were shards of glass and pottery. Furniture was overturned and a briny, musty smell of the sea filled the air, a stench of decay and emptiness.

Oh, for my sister's neatness!

I checked the food locker—it was in the first-floor parlor—where bread and cheese were normally stored. The bread was like an old, wet sponge, the cheese equally unappetizing. I found a withered apple, took a bite, only to spit it out. It tasted like seaweed. Moreover, since nothing makes one hungrier than a failed attempt at eating, I was now ravenous.

I set up one of the chairs, picked up some broken glass, and then wandered aimlessly into my father's office yet again, as if somehow he might have returned. Of course, he had not.

As I stood there, I remembered something of great importance: Father kept a small money-box under his bed. Made of wood, leather-bound, it was always closed by means of a large padlock. Opening it was, of course, strictly against house laws, forbidden upon pain of severe punishment.

Surely, my father would not want me to starve. I had

to eat something, and that meant purchasing something, which in turn required money.

Hesitating—to go against my father's rules was not easy—I dropped to my knees, reached under the bed, and drew forth the box.

The first thing I observed was that the padlock was unfastened. Had my father left it open for me? Even then I paused to acknowledge that to turn back the lid might be the wrong thing to do.

Should I or should I not open the box?

Uncomfortable, but telling myself I must have some money to buy food so I could remain in the house, I threw back the lid and looked inside.

CHAPTER SEVEN

My Father's Money-Box and What It Led To.

The box was empty.

One moment I was disappointed that there was nothing to take. The next I felt relieved that I could not take what was forbidden. Unfortunately, that did nothing to lessen my anxiety or hunger.

Unsoothed, I went back outside and picked up two chimney bricks and set them down neatly. As I gazed upon a forecourt full of debris, I was quickly overwhelmed by what I would have to do to put things right.

Suddenly wishing to get away from the house, I walked the two streets that brought me to the Weymouth Bay shore. It was a wide, sweeping curve of sandy beach, a place where my friends and I often played. Unfortunately none were there. No doubt they were attending to their injured homes.

As I stood there, foaming waves made a soft whooshing as the water flowed high only to retreat. Above, squawking seagulls flew by, while one or two walked along the beach edge, pecking at the sand. This sand was most often soft underfoot. That morning the storm's pelting rain had made it hard and crusty.

Overhead, the sky was dull gray and a cold, damp breeze was coming in. The gray-blue sea stretched far, roiled with heaving, foam-crested waves. In the distance, the topmost sails of a ship moved slowly east, to London, perhaps. Where my father and sister were. To the south was the hooked Weymouth peninsula that protected the harbor. No one was there.

I felt abandoned and unaided.

At that moment I was sure there was nothing for me to do but wait for my father's return—whenever that might be. Which is to say I could not leave Melcombe. I didn't even consider it. Besides, I had no way to do so.

But as I gazed about I realized there was a trail of footsteps in the sand, leading eastward and westward. I even saw wagon-wheel ruts. The imprints were softened, suggesting they had been made when the storm was still in progress, or perhaps when it was weakening.

Not wanting to return to an empty house, having nothing better to do, and glad to have some purpose, though idle, I set off along the beach and followed the foot marks. I walked like an old man, eyes cast down, stepping slowly. As I went, my thoughts returned to what Mrs. Grady suggested: I would be sent to the poorhouse. The notion upset me greatly, enough to put my mind on how to avoid that.

It was only after I had walked along the beach for about a mile, thoroughly lost in my tangle of grievesome thoughts, that I looked up. To my surprise, something huge lay right before me.

At first, I was so taken aback I could not make out what I was seeing. Then I realized it was a ship lying on the beach. But oddly, which explains my lack of perception, she was careened over to one side. This is to say her deck was perpendicular to the beach, her keel completely exposed. I did see two masts, or rather, what remained of them, two splintered stumps. She was a brig.

A moment's thought made it perfectly clear what had happened: the storm had snapped her masts and then flung the brig ashore. As for the many footprints that led directly to and from her, they meant one of two things: The crew had fled to town for safety. Or people from town had gone to the ship and looted her.

This was not unusual. Famously, when ships were wrecked near Melcombe Regis or Weymouth—or anywhere along the Dorset coast—they were ransacked by locals for anything of value. My father was often engaged in attempts to recover what had been stolen. Just as often, he was employed to protect those who had been falsely charged with looting. In such matters was the origin of his frequent clashes with the port's customs master, Mr. Bartholomew.

It was because of my father's work that I knew if there were survivors of a wreck, they had all rights to the ship and cargo, and no one should touch her. But if the ship had no survivors, what was called a "dead wreck," people believed they could take what they fancied. That said, going upon a wrecked ship—even out of mere curiosity—was absolutely against the law.

Moving slowly, looking for signs of life, I drew closer to the vessel. Once alongside, she seemed large, old, and exceedingly weathered. When I circled about I saw a name across her stern, *The Rose in June*. She was then an English brig. More important, I saw no signs of life.

How long, I wondered, had the ship been on the beach? What happened to the crew? Had they drowned? Did any survive? Had they wandered off when the ship was washed ashore? Would anyone be back soon?

I saw a gaping hole on her hull, which apparently had been smashed in. This might have happened when tossed ashore. Or, it could have been made by looters, the easier to remove the cargo. That, I knew, was a hanging offence.

I circled back around. The brig was careened so far

over that even while standing on the beach, I could see the entire deck.

"Hallo!" I shouted. There was no response.

The more I gazed at the deck, the more I realized that there was not one metal fitting remaining. Block and tackle, gone. At the helm of the ship, higher than the main deck, I could see the place where the steering wheel should have been attached. It, too, was gone.

It was easy to see what happened: the ship had been stripped bare of everything of value. The looters must have come early. Knowing the Crown official— Mr. Bartholomew—would not come to the ship until after the tempest, the looters probably came during the storm. Such gross theft also explained the wagon ruts: a cart would have been required to haul everything away.

Unable to restrain my curiosity, I reached up, and with ease, crawled over the gunnel and set myself on the deck planking. The brig was so lopsided I was able to stand upright upon the inner bulwark.

Amidships, which was over my head, I spied an open hatch. It would lead, I knew, to the hold, the cargo, and the crew's quarters. Perhaps someone was down there in need of help. Let it also be admitted that it occurred to me that something of value may have been left.

As for what happened next, let me lead you through the sensibleness of my thought: If I had some money, or something of value, then I would not be considered poor. Not being poor, I would not be sent to the poorhouse. That would mean I could wait for my father to return. Finally, it was perfectly clear to me that other people had already taken things from the ship. Very well then: Why should I not do as much and thereby save myself?

Such was my logic.

I looked back toward town. No one was on the beach.

But what if—I did ask myself—the crew or other would-be looters came back? Surely, at some point Mr. Bartholomew would come out to claim the wreck. That was how the law did its work.

Should I go on her or not?

CHAPTER EIGHT

A Short Chapter with Long Consequences.

What harm, I told myself, could there be in merely inspecting *The Rose in June*? To be sure, not strictly legal—but I would do nothing beyond that. That much I swore to myself.

To get to that hatch I had to climb over the bulwarks, then pull myself upward. Happily, the caulking—the oakum stuffed between planks to make ships watertight—had sprung away, leaving gaps between the warped planking into which my fingers could take purchase.

When I reached the hatch, I drew myself yet higher until I could peer down inside. There was some light below, perhaps because of the hole in the hull. The light enabled me to see steps leading down. Because the ship lay so awkwardly, these steps extended directly out and away from me.

Let it be admitted: The more I peered, the more I desired to go below. Still, I vacillated. It was not merely dangerous; my legal apprenticeship had taught me something: to go any farther on an abandoned ship was prohibited. What if someone came along and I was discovered?

Against that possibility I admitted that if I found food, or money, it would be the saving of me, surely a good thing. The next moment I told myself that everything of value was probably taken.

Despite these contradictions, I hoisted myself higher even as I glanced back nervously along the beach, east and west. No one was visible. Convinced I was not observed, I swung my legs over the open hatch and inched forward, until my feet dangled. Then I moved up even farther, until I was sitting on the lip of the hatch, using one hand to hold on to the edge, so as to keep from descending too fast.

With a sudden snap, the wood I was clinging to broke away. Frantic, I tried to grasp something. It was too late. The weight of my body carried me down, so that I plummeted straight into the shadowy hold of *The Rose in June*.

CHAPTER NINE

In the Hold of The Rose in June, *and What Happened There.*

Down I tumbled, head over heels, topsy-turvy, until I landed on the outer bulwarks of the lower deck. I struck with such a jarring thump the air went from my body, the sight from my eyes. For some moments I lay still, my back hurting, my head muddled, and the stench of rotting fish so strong it made me want to retch.

To make matters worse, the ship lay so oddly it took time to orient myself. It did not help that the light was darkful. Such feeble illumination as there was came from the open hatch, as well as from the hole on the far side of the ship's hull, above where I lay.

I was sprawled in such a way that I was facing the floor of the lower deck. Empty and broken wooden boxes, as well as staved-in barrels, had been tossed about. Nearby, two benches lay at odd angles. Before me was a table, but it must have been attached to the floor, because I was looking at its top surface. Of course, nothing was on it.

Off to my right, toward the ship's stern, was a wall in which a door had been set. The door was attached to the frame by only one hinge, which left the door hanging skewed. This entryway appeared to lead to a cabin. Being at the helm, I supposed it must belong to the ship's captain.

Opposite, toward the bow of the ship, was another wall, with yet another opening, but no door. That entry, I assumed, led to the fo'c'sle, the crew's quarters.

As I gazed about, I saw a few dead, dull-eyed fish. The bareness of everything else proved what I already supposed: looters had been there and had completely stripped *The Rose in June*.

Even so, I did not move, but continued to remain where I had fallen. Mrs. Grady's words, "You'll be grateful for the poorhouse, which will take care of you with kindness," flowed back into my head like a rising tide.

Perhaps, I thought, something of value had been left by the looters. Did I not advise you, in this book's subtitle, that I would tell you of my follies? Well then, as I lay there, my fear of the poorhouse was greater than my fear of any punishment the law might inflict on me for looting.

I told myself this: I shall be quick and if I take anything, it shall be only of the smallest worth, just enough to keep me out of the poorhouse. What's more, I made a solemn vow—hand on heart, eyes to Heaven—that when my father returned, I would return the worth of anything I took.

I beg you: put yourself in my circumstance. English law, as I often had heard my father say, was only about the protection of property. I was thinking about protecting myself. I had yet to experience the old saying: He who has suffered little, suffers most when little things happen.

I pushed myself into an upright position, so that I stood with my back against the inside bulwark of the ship. The possibility of finding anything valuable in the crew's cabin was slight. So I moved step-by-step in the direction of what I assumed was the captain's cabin, where I would most likely find something of substance. Since the entryway to the captain's cabin was above my head, I had to grasp the door's frame and haul myself up. Once my chin was over the frame I peered inside.

What I saw was a small table attached to the floor and a bed set into the wall, but nothing else. Cupboards, doors open, were bare. Closets had been stripped. Even bedclothes were gone.

Once again, I felt relieved, just as I had felt when opening my father's money-box. With nothing to steal, I could not be a thief. Not being a thief, I considered myself full of virtue.

My thoughts now turned to getting away from the

ship as fast as possible. Reversing myself, I started back to where I had first fallen and then tried to determine how I was going to climb back to the top deck.

No sooner had I decided that I would have to go out by way of the hole in the hull—no matter how awkwardly placed; it was above my head—when I heard voices. I had no idea what they were saying; enough to know that people were close to the ship, and therefore me.

Not wanting to be discovered, I glanced about, altogether agitated. I had been to the captain's cabin and knew there was no place for me to hide there. My eyes turned forward, the crew's quarters.

As fast as I could, I inched along the bulwark, until I came to the fo'c'sle's opening. As before, I hauled myself up and peered into the crew's cabin. All the while, I was hearing those voices drawing ever nearer.

Within the crew's cabin, I saw a series of what appeared to be shelves, six of them, three on either bulwark, stacked one atop the other, with about three feet between them. I realized they were the berths, where the crew slept. When I saw that these berths were close together—rather like a bookcase—and that it was hard to see deep within them, I decided I'd found the perfect place to hide.

Those voices urged me on.

I hoisted myself up and crawled through the door. Once on the far side I let myself down. Trying desperately to go fast without noise, I reached the lowest berth, rolled into it, and fairly dropped down where it was most murky. There I lay, trying not to move while keeping the sounds of my breathing to a minimum.

The voices grew louder. Then came footsteps. Whoever the people were, they had come upon the ship. Were they the crew? Were they looters? For all I knew they might have been boys like me, even friends. But what if they were officials? Some magistrate like Mr. Bartholomew, the Crown's customs master?

In the end, I did not care who they were. Determined to outlast them, I remained still.

Gradually, my eyes grew accustomed to such light as there was. That's when I realized there was something affixed to the wood directly above me. If the ship had been properly pitched, it would have been under whoever had been sleeping in the berth, perhaps beneath a thin mattress. It took me some time to determine what I was seeing: a folded packet of dark cloth.

Though it drew my intense interest, I dared not make motions to touch it, much less take it into hand, fearful I would attract attention by some sound, however slight.

After I am not sure how long, the footsteps and voices finally diminished until I was convinced that whoever had been on the ship had gone off. Only then did I allow myself to turn my thoughts back to the cloth packet.

Easy enough to reach up and touch it. Not so easy to pull free. It was tacked to the wood, meant to remain there. Nonetheless, I kept poking about, trying to gain a hold. As I worked, I told myself that the sailor whose packet this was most likely had drowned, and therefore had no need for whatever was there. Finally, I gained a grip, yanked, so the packet came free only to have it split apart and shower me with shillings.

First I was startled. Then I was elated: I would be able to take care of myself. I could stay in our house and await Father's return. I could avoid the poorhouse.

No sooner did those happy ideas come into my head than the cautionary story my father so often told us also came—to wit, that nine-year-old boy who had stolen two pennies' worth of paint and was hanged for his wrongdoing.

I counted the shillings. Some thirty shillings! A fortune!

Then I checked myself. I was about to take many shillings. Since each shilling was worth twelve pennies, by taking them I put myself in grave danger.

Thus my dilemma: If I did not take the money, I might well be sent to the poorhouse. If I did take it and my theft was discovered, I might be hanged.

The question was therefore stark: Should I, or should I not, take the shillings?

CHAPTER TEN

The Decision I Made and the Consequences That Followed.

Because I feared being sent to the poorhouse, I took the money but not all—only twenty-three shillings. That amount, I decided, would allow me to stay in our house until my father's return.

Why not all? I guessed how much I would need to feed myself and would take no more than necessity required. Such was my sense of virtue.

So resolved, it required considerable twisting and turning upon that narrow berth before I managed to gather all the coins. Contorting myself further, I managed to put what I was taking into my trouser pocket.

I left the rest.

What followed was the laborious process of getting out

of the narrow berth. That too required strength and agility. Next, I climbed out of the ship's hold onto the main deck. From there it was easy—one hand thrust into my pocket so as not to lose the taken shillings, to step off the ship and return to the beach.

Excited by newfound security, anxious to get home, I set out with high vigor. Happily, the shore still appeared deserted. As it happened, it didn't remain that way. As I moved closer to town, I saw someone coming along the sands, moving in my direction.

Regrettably, it did not take long for me to realize that the person advancing was none other than Mr. Bartholomew, Melcombe Regis and Weymouth's customs master. He was followed close on by a servant.

Let it be said that out of all the people whom I might have met at such a time and place, the worst was Mr. Bartholomew, my father's principal enemy and antagonist. Yet it must also be said, he was most logically there, for as customs master, he had the Crown's responsibility to protect dead wrecks by making a government claim to *The Rose in June.*

According to my father, Mr. Bartholomew had paid—as was common—a goodly price to get this post, but made a grasping-handed use of it. Father insisted that the customs master was no better than the smugglers he arrested and voiced this opinion publicly. You may be sure Mr. Bartholomew reacted with indignation to these accusations.

Whether my father was right or not, if Mr. Bartholomew discovered that I—or anyone—had stolen anything from the wrecked ship—so much as a rusty nail—his considerable legal powers were such that he could arrest me without delay, fine me—pocketing the fine—and have me hanged. Thus, though I had gotten off the ship just in time, I had money in my pocket—taken from the ship—which put me in jeopardy.

That was not all. You will recall that my father was in the habit of playing backgammon at the Golden Lion Inn, betting large sums. One of his principal opponents was this same Mr. Bartholomew. As I had been informed, they had played the night Father disappeared. Whereas my father won far more often than he lost, Mr. Bartholomew was in the habit of losing, which made him dislike my father with great intensity. To lose at games to someone you detest is a gross mortification. Father often said that a man should be known not by his friends but by his enemies. And I was about to meet his biggest enemy in the most compromising situation.

Since it is quite common for young people to believe adults have almost uncanny powers, I feared Mr. Bartholomew would know what I had done. I therefore thrust a hand deep into the pocket where I had put the coins, in hopes he would think it was my hand that caused the lump.

In short, if ever there was a moment for false smiles that was it. *Do not act guilty,* I told myself.

Mr. Bartholomew was a large man with a rough and rosy face, with thick black eyebrows—swept up and oiled—so as to give him a look of animosity. Old-fashioned in appearance, he was wearing a shoulder-length white gooseberry wig and a large three-cornered hat, the blue brim turned up on three sides.

He had on a blue waistcoat with silver buttons and lace trim, yellow breeches, and white stockings; over all, a dark cloak. His shoes were black, fastened by big silver buckles. In his right hand was an elegant walking stick capped with ivory. From his waistcoat hung a short sword, the kind called a hanger. As I hope to suggest, he was a man who liked to dress so as to proclaim his great self-esteem and office.

His regular facial features were severe, ever ready to judge the world. When he recognized me, he stopped short and those features became infused with considerable anger. Even as he lifted his stick, suggesting he might strike me down, he lowered his eyebrows to increase his look of ferocity.

His servant was a young man dressed like a Jack-a-dandy, that is, in an elegant uniform, with a haughty face that bore an imposing mustache—curled-up ends—such as I had rarely seen. It added to the look of contempt he bestowed on me.

"Good morning, Master Pitts," Mr. Bartholomew greeted me loudly, but speaking slowly, as if I was an underwit and he needed to pronounce something of importance. He even lowered his stick and leaned on it, so that he might stand a little taller. His bulk was such that the stick bowed.

"Good morning, sir," I said, with a bob of a bend while I struggled to keep a smiley face.

"Have you been out to see the dead wreck?" he asked, his eyes charged with allegation.

I saw no harm in admitting to seeing it, so I said, "Yes, sir, I've seen it."

"You did not get on her, I trust."

"Oh, no, sir," I said. "I wouldn't do that. I know better."

"Under the Wrecking Offences," he nonetheless informed me, "merely entering a dead wreck without permission means twelve months in gaol. Should you carry off any goods, you would forfeit triple their value. Or," he scowled, "be hanged. Let it be understood"—he lifted his stick and poked my chest, as if to skewer me—"it does not matter how young you are."

"Yes, sir. I know." Impulsively, I pulled my hand from my pocket and held out two empty palms.

"I have been informed," said Mr. Bartholomew, "that the ship has already been looted."

"I wouldn't know, sir," I said, struggling to present myself as innocent as a minnow, all the while smiling in what I hoped was a guileless way. "I was only looking at her from the beach." Even as I spoke it was not merely the shillings in my pocket that grew warm, but my face.

The mustachioed servant snorted in contempt.

As for Mr. Bartholomew, he continued to look at me with a condemnatory stare as if to catch me out. "I sincerely hope you are not given to telling lies—like your father."

"Sir?"

"We were playing backgammon last night at the Golden Lion. In two words, your father is a liar and a cheat. I should add a third word: a cackling cheat."

"I don't wish to think so, sir."

"When I left the tables," continued Mr. Bartholomew, "I sent him a note telling him that I considered him a scoundrel and that I intend to bring legal charges against him."

I guessed that must have been one of the letters my father had been given.

"But now," Mr. Bartholomew went on, "I have been informed that the whereabouts of your father is unknown."

That Mr. Bartholomew was already aware that my

father had disappeared meant that many people knew it. As the saying goes, "A small town has large eyes."

"I suspect," suggested Mr. Bartholomew, "he fled out of shame and cowardice thereby acknowledging his crime."

"Sir," I returned, "I believe my father is an honest man."

"Your face suggests that you may be honest," replied Mr. Bartholomew. "But as it is oft said, 'Like father, like son.' As for his disappearance, would you prefer to think he met with some misfortune in the storm?"

"Oh, no, sir! I believe he'll return home very soon," I said, only wishing it was so.

"I sincerely hope your father has survived," said the customs master. "Because as soon as I locate him I intend to drag him to the magistrate at the guild hall and charge him with fraud. I shall not be happy until I see your father in prison."

"Will you really do that, sir?" I asked, trying to keep my smile though my distress increased.

"I shall. I will enjoy exposing him as the scoundrel he is. Do you know the penalty for his crime?"

"No, sir."

For the first time the servant spoke: "Transportation to the colonies. Hard labor for at least seven years." It was as if he was reading the law for his master.

Mr. Bartholomew said, "I am determined to remove

your father from England. When he returns be so good as to tell him that." Then, sarcastically quoting my father, he added, "'The law is king.' Now, step aside; I must go on to my official duties."

Mr. Bartholomew strode by me in the direction of the ship. His servant did not even deign to look at me.

I watched them go. Was this not more distressing news? I had learned the content of one of those letters my father had received: He had been accused of cheating! Threatened with arrest! And transportation!

I knew Father gambled and that he won far more often than he lost. In that regard, I kept in mind something he once told me: "When those who lose at life suffer defeat at cards or other games, they would rather accuse the winner of cheating than acknowledge their own weak play."

But what if Father was guilty and, under the threat of terrible punishment he had fled, as Mr. Bartholomew claimed?

What came into my head was that it was urgent for me to find a way to warn Father that he should not come home. But how could I? I had no idea where in London he might be. Did not my father tell me that London was a "monstrous" city?

No, I should not go there, but must remain home so that the moment he stepped through our door I could alert him to his danger.

CHAPTER ELEVEN

Which Concerns a Letter I Could Not Read.

I fled home. Once there the first thing I did was to pull the front door shut, so as not to be observed. Next, I cast about trying to decide where I could hide the money.

As I searched, I noticed that piece of paper, the one that I had discovered under the lantern when I first awoke in the morning and came down the steps. It had been sodden wet and impossible to read but in the time I had been gone from the house it had dried.

I picked it up and now saw it was in my father's hand and that it was a letter to me. He must have come home the night before, found me asleep, written the missive, and left in haste. That said, at first glance the writing made no sense.

I herewith present his note just as I saw it with XXXs

where I could not understand the words because the writing was smeared during the storm.

OlivXX,

I XXXXXXXd X XXXXXX which informed me that Charity XX XXXXX XX be mXXXXXd!! This is XXXXXXXX XXXs. I intend to XXXX XX. I leave XXX XXXXXn immediately. I will XXXXX mXXXX for XXX with XX WXXXXX at the XXXXXX LXXX XXXXX X XXXX XXX XXXXX. You XXX apply XX XXX for such XXXXX as you XXXX.

I shall XXXXXX when X XXX.

Your XXXXXX,

GXXXXXX PXXXX

I cannot tell you how many times I reread the letter trying to gain some understanding, attempting to fill in the smudged parts with letters and words. I could make out some; OlivXX meant Oliver; GXXXXXX PXXXX meant Gabriel Pitts. But what did mXXXXXd mean as it pertained to Charity? Mistreated? Maligned? Murdered?

Though it troubled me greatly, I could not fathom it.

The most I could surmise was that my father had learned some dreadful news about Charity that required him to go immediately to London on her behalf. Nothing,

59

as far as I could tell, about being accused of cheating, the charge that Mr. Bartholomew had leveled against him.

As for what he meant by the sentence that contained the words "I intend to . . ." I had no idea.

While it was extremely distressing to learn that Charity was in difficulty—"mXXXXXd!!"—it was a comfort to know Father had gone to her aid. I was even prepared to forgive him for not letting me know aforehand. In a sense his letter suggested he had informed me. In any case, I folded the letter and put it in my pocket, intending to untangle its message later.

Since I had gained no knowledge as to when my father might return, there remained the question of what I should do. I was convinced that having money meant I would not be taken to the poorhouse. That said, I was equally sure I must not display my newfound wealth too quickly. People would wonder how I got it, the more so if Mrs. Grady repeated what I had said, that I had no money.

Thinking that way, it was not hard to decide where to put the shillings: in my father's money-box. I dragged the box out from under the bed, and deposited the coins there.

No sooner did I do that than I worried in my state of disquiet that if anyone searched for my money—which in my current circumstances, I considered possible—I would need a safer place. Besides, the money-box padlock was gone.

After considerable shilly-shallying, I chose the hearth as a hiding place, knowing that with our chimney gone, there would be no fires lit there. It seemed, moreover, an unlikely place for anyone to look.

I retrieved the shillings from the money-box, located a flint box, lit a candle, and stepped inside the hearth. Since I was much smaller than the hearth, I was able to stand inside the flue.

Holding the candle up, I studied the stones by which the flue had been constructed a long time ago. At a higher level than my head, I discovered where a stone had fallen out, leaving a niche, like a shelf.

I placed the candle on the ground, so as to have some light, and put the money in my pocket. It proved a simple matter for me to climb up the flue—using the jagged interior stones as steps—and perch myself on high. Then I stacked the coins in the niche. Having done that, and emerging from the fireplace, I had a sense of relief and safety.

I was also exhausted. Since breakfasting at the Golden Lion Inn, I had eaten nothing. When I returned to the larder there was that bread, but it was in no better condition. I tried the cheese, and while barely eatable, I consumed it anyway. I was too tired to go out and purchase food.

Instead, I wandered through the house, trying to find a place I might rest. The driest spot was my sister's room and bed. I flopped down and lay there, letter in hand, trying to make sense of "mXXXXXd." Had Charity been misunderstood, muddled, misplaced? At some point I fell asleep and slept through the night and did not waken till morning when I heard a pounding on the front door.

Stuffing my father's letter into my pocket, I hurried down and opened the door. Two men were standing there, Mr. Ebenezer Bicklet and Mr. Jeremiah Turnsall. Mr. Bicklet was a churchwarden. Mr. Turnsall was the town's overseer of the poor.

Which is to say, I was being visited by the two men in charge of Melcombe's children's poorhouse.

CHAPTER TWELVE

In Which I Experience the Kindness of Adults Toward Children.

Mr. Bicklet was a churchwarden connected to Christchurch, the primary Church of England institution in Melcombe. He was a rather small, dainty man, his movements forever rapid and jerky, like a blackbird that constantly shifts his head to make sure he sees and hears all. Mr. Bicklet's small hands seemed to flutter, wing-like. He did not stride so much as he took small, delicate, almost hopping steps. Even his pointy nose was beak-like, forever pecking into things and people.

My father, being a Nonconformist in matters of faith—among many other things—disputed religion with Mr. Bicklet, and did so loudly, hotly, and publicly. The truth is he liked to mock the man.

As for Mr. Turnsall, though equally short, he was thick

and puffy, with sagging cheeks, rather thick lips, and bulging eyes. His short brown wig was like a cork on a jug, being too small for his globose head. His bulksome hands dangled from the sleeves of his too small jacket. With knees like lumpy potatoes and ankles like turnips, he put in mind too many knobby vegetables stuffed into a small sack.

What is more, my father had brought Mr. Turnsall to court, claiming he had made excessive profits from his role as overseer of Melcombe's children's poorhouse.

My encounter with Mr. Bartholomew on the beach made it clear that the town knew my father was gone and that I had been left alone. I had the kindly, if gossipy Mrs. Grady to thank for that, though 'twas my fault to have spoken.

In other words, the two men at my door were among my father's many foes, and they had come, I was sure, to do me mischief. I felt, as I had not before, the reason Charity wanted to leave home.

Mr. Bicklet spoke first. "Good morning, Master Pitts, is your father at home?"

Sure he knew the answer, I put on my cheerful, smiley face so as to suggest all was well and said, "No, sir."

"Will he be back soon?" asked Mr. Turnsall.

"I expect him, yes, sir," said I. This was not entirely a lie, since I did not say when I expected him back. At some point surely my father would return. I just did not know when.

"Would you be kind enough to allow us to enter and wait for him?" said Mr. Bicklet.

Groping for a way to deal with the situation, I said, "Please, sirs, I would invite you in, but I fear the house is in a great disorder because of the recent storm. Even our chimney has tumbled."

"Many a house has been affected," said Mr. Turnsall. "It's sad how much has been destroyed." He didn't sound sad.

"Consider it the judgment of the Lord," said Mr. Bicklet. "Therefore, you may be sure that your home will not be an embarrassment to us since we are charitable men. So, may we come in and wait for your father's return?"

It is hard for a boy to resist two grown men; men, moreover, of considerable authority. Not knowing how to keep them out, I stepped aside.

When they entered the house Mr. Turnsall stood and stared at the general chaos, while Mr. Bicklet hopped about prying into every little thing, his fingers lifting, shifting, and examining all that lay about. I will admit, seeing the house with their eyes, so to speak, it was very messy.

"It's bad, isn't it?" I said, gesturing to the chairs. "Even these are muddy." I spoke in hopes they would not sit down and thereby shorten their stay.

The two men remained silent, frowning, looking about, as if taking inventory—or making a judgment.

Mr. Bicklet pointed to my father's room. "Is that your father's cabinet?"

"Yes, sir, it is," I said, only then realizing I'd left the money-box open on the desk. Without my permission, the churchwarden took quick steps into the room and gazed about. I even saw him peer into the money-box. At the same moment, Mr. Turnsall ascended the stairs.

I placed myself near the hearth to protect the hidden money.

The two men returned to the front room. It was Mr. Turnsall, coming down from above, who said, "This house is not habitable." He did not say this to me, but to Mr. Bicklet.

"I presume," Mr. Bicklet said to me, "your father has seen the condition of the house."

I thought it best to say nothing.

"Do you have food?" asked Mr. Turnsall.

"Yes, sir," I said, but chose not to speak of the food's condition.

Mr. Bicklet was too quick for me. "Please show it to us," he said.

I pointed to the box larder across the room.

Mr. Turnsall lifted the lid, stared down, sniffed, frowned, and announced, "It's unfit for consumption."

To me, Mr. Bicklet said, "How will you purchase food?"

Trying to dodge his question, I said, "Please, sirs, I have money."

Mr. Turnsall said, "I heard otherwise."

To which Mr. Bicklet added, "I suppose that was your father's money-box in his room. It was bare. Please show us the money you have."

As you, my reader, know, I did have money. You also know how I got it and where I put it, or rather hid it. In an instant, I realized that if I retrieved the money, these men would most likely ask why the shillings were up the chimney. It would have been hard to explain. On the other hand, if I showed them nothing, they would more than likely drag me off to the poorhouse as a penniless and abandoned child.

I thought of a further problem. If I revealed the money to them and they, with their adult authority, took it, I would have no means of surviving until my father returned.

I don't know how long it took for these thoughts to pass through my head, but an impatient Mr. Turnsall said, "Can you show us the money?"

Forced into a decision, I said, "No, sir," at which point the two men exchanged a meaningful look.

I am of the belief that when two adults exchange a meaningful look in the presence of a child, there is little doubt that the adults will have nothing pleasing to say to that child.

"Very well, young man," pronounced Mr. Bicklet. "It has come to our attention that your father, Mr. Pitts, took the coach for London just before the storm."

"Did you know that?" Mr. Turnsall asked me bluntly.

"Oh yes, sir," I said, offering my best smile, so as to suggest it was of little importance.

"Do you know why he went?"

My father's smudged letter seemed to positively crackle in my pocket. Since I had no intention of telling the two men that my sister might be in some kind of trouble, or that Mr. Bartholomew was about to file a complaint against my father, I remained mum.

"Since your father has gone to London," continued Mr. Turnsall, "it is more than likely that he will be gone for at least ten days, probably more."

"Moreover," added Mr. Bicklet, "this house is not livable."

"And you have no food."

"Or money."

"Now then," said Mr. Turnsall, "how old are you?"

"Twelve, sir."

Mr. Bicklet cocked his head in my direction and considered me with his bird-like eyes. "I think," he pronounced, "you are much younger."

"Truly, sir," I protested. "I am twelve."

"Can you prove it?" said Mr. Turnsall.

That question was perhaps one of the most frustrating demands ever put to me. What child—any child—can provide proof of his or her age? Do we have the papers, certificates, evidence? Could you, dear reader, right now, on demand, prove your age? Oh, how I regretted not going to Mr. Buffin and getting a document that confirmed my age.

"I believe," said Mr. Bicklet, "you are not even eight years of age."

"But—"

"I'm sure you are right," said Mr. Turnsall to Mr. Bicklet, not to me. "In case you didn't know," Mr. Turnsall went on to me, "the recent Poor Law states that any abandoned child under the age of eleven shall be sent to the parish poorhouse. When you turn eight, you will be apprenticed."

"Please, sir, I am already apprenticed."

"To whom?"

"My father. I'm learning the law."

Mr. Bicklet could not suppress a pipping squeak. "Ah yes, 'the law is king.' Very well!" said he. "Let Mr. Pitts come forward and prove it."

What could I say? Nothing.

Mr. Bicklet turned to Mr. Turnsall. "Do you know the father of this boy?"

"A meddlesome Nonconformist lawyer, who is forever harassing me as to what and what is not lawful," responded

Mr. Turnsall. "He has accused me of getting more than my share of fair rewards for overseeing the poorhouse."

To which Mr. Bicklet replied, "He never stops insulting the rightful religion of England, which I represent. I've come to believe Mr. Pitts is one of those dreadful Levelers, a radical who will destroy property and seek to make all men equal. A stiff-rumped clink-clank. And what has he done? He has abandoned his child. Shameful!"

"Therefore," said Mr. Turnsall to me, "as the delegated authorities of Melcombe Regis, we shall do you, Oliver Cromwell Pitts, the great kindness of bringing you to the children's poorhouse so that we may care for you. When, and if your father returns, he can legally claim you, and do with you as he wishes. 'The law is king.' Until such a time it is our duty to take care of you. You may herewith consider us your legal guardians. Now then, come along."

So there it was, these men were going to punish me as a way of striking at my father.

Knowing there was no way I could resist, I quickly made a plan. I would not resist going with them. Instead I would wait at the poorhouse for my father to return. I even supposed I could save money, for it was my understanding that one was fed in the children's poorhouse.

It seemed a suitable, easy plan. What in fact happened, you are about to learn.

CHAPTER THIRTEEN

In Which I Am Enrolled in the Children's Poorhouse.

I had not been arrested. No one had discovered—as far as I knew—that I had taken those shillings from the wreck of *The Rose in June*. Nor did Mr. Bicklet or Mr. Turnsall so much as lay a finger on me. I was not forced to go with them. All of which is to say, as far as I was concerned, my going to the children's poorhouse was my clever plan to stay in Melcombe cheaply.

The Melcombe Regis Children's Parish Poorhouse was located at the corner of Petticoat Lane and West Street. The building stood at a right angle to what is called the Back Harborside, the bay where ships, after unloading their cargoes at the river docks, could anchor safely. It was not an elegant part of town. Nor will it surprise you when

I tell you that I, who never believed I would have anything to do with the poorhouse, had never looked at it closely before.

A plain stone structure of two floors, it had small windows, five on the upper floor, four on the first floor, on either side of a central doorway. There was a chimney at either end. The building seemed not to have suffered destruction from the storm, but then it was farther away from the sea. All in all, it appeared as a stolid, dreary, and lifeless structure that most likely had been a military barrack.

Mr. Bicklet tapped on the door. It was opened shortly by a girl who could not have been more than six years of age dressed in a plain gray smock. Her pasty pale face was not altogether clean and, despite her youth, her brow was creased with worry lines.

Seeing Mr. Bicklet, she curtsied.

"Yes, sir?" she whispered, as if afraid to talk too loudly.

"Is Master Probert at home?" inquired Mr. Bicklet. "We are bringing him an abandoned boy."

The girl glanced at me. What passed over her face, I thought, was not so much sympathy as pity. Whether it was because I had been abandoned or because I was coming to the children's poorhouse, or if she was asking for pity for herself, it was impossible to guess.

"Yes, please, sirs," she said, small voiced. "Please enter."

With a harsh prod on my shoulder, the two gentlemen

and I stepped into a vestibule. The girl shut the door behind us and quickly fled through a door on the left and disappeared.

Aside from being fed in the poorhouse, I had thought that it would be a much warmer place than my own wrecked home. In fact, it was not merely gloomy, but cold and damp. Moreover, we were confronted by a high desk, and behind that desk, perched on a stool, was a tall man. It was as if he was guarding the door, but whether to keep people in or out, I could not at that moment say.

As far as I could see, the man had a narrow face and a well-shaved if small chin almost blue in hue. His eyes, under string-thin eyebrows, were small and sharp, his nose large and lengthy, whereas his mouth seemed hardly more than a lipless slit, not shaped to convey merriment.

He wore a wig that was glossy black in color, with crisp curls at his ears. The jacket he wore was equally black, high buttoned, and shiny, more shell-like than cloth. All in all he rather put me in mind of those insects one saw about the dock area, a cockroach.

He was writing in a massive book with a black-feathered quill in his right hand. His left hand, with long, narrow fingers, hung over the forward edge of the desk, and clutched a ring of keys. On his desk was a tall candlestick, its flame like a small, yellow eye. An hourglass also perched there. Near his feet was an iron pot, which glowed, suggesting it contained hot coals to provide some heat, at least for him.

As he sat there this man gently patted his wig, whether to make sure it was there or out of vanity, I had no idea. When he finally looked up at us, his narrow mouth seemed to compress even more, so that any smile might be bitten, chewed, and swallowed before it had the temerity to reveal itself.

"Ah! Mr. Bicklet," he said in a voice that was as slow as it was raspy, rather like a dull saw. "Mr. Turnsall. You are most welcome, gentlemen."

"Mr. Probert, sir," said Mr. Turnsall. "Pleased to see you looking so well, sir."

"I am very well," returned Mr. Probert, in a manner that conveyed he truly thought excellent things of himself. "To what do I owe the pleasure of your company?"

"Sir," said Mr. Turnsall, "Mr. Bicklet and I have discovered an abandoned and impoverished boy in need of your care and kindness. We rescued him from the storm and worse." He pushed me forward.

"You gentlemen have always been extremely kind and full of charity," said Mr. Probert even as he fixed his eyes on me with a gaze that was full of hostility, as if I were at fault. "I can see that this boy is unfortunate in his life but fortunate that you have rescued him." He patted his wig, as if to suggest that he was not unfortunate.

"To make matters worse," said Mr. Turnsall, "he has a rascal of a father who, I fear, in the midst of last night's storm, abandoned him."

"And who, I must ask, is this negligent father?"

"The lawyer, Mr. Gabriel Pitts."

"Mr. Pitts!" cried Mr. Probert. "I know him only too well." He patted his wig again, and that time I was sure it was meant to convey his dignity in contrast to my father. "Mr. Pitts has nosed about this institution, and has been critical of our good works. He has actually accused me of mistreating the children under my care. He may be described, at best, as vicious vermin."

Hearing these words, my heart sank. Here was yet another of my father's adversaries.

"That's much the man," agreed Mr. Bicklet.

"A dangerous troublemaker," added Mr. Turnsall. "Known for his belligerence."

"And now," put in Mr. Bicklet, "he has abandoned his son."

They spoke with glee.

Mr. Probert gazed at me anew. "Then I am delighted that we can help his boy grow up so that he at least shall be a benefit to our community."

He leaned forward over his desk. "Boy, what is your Christian name?"

"Oliver Cromwell, sir."

Mr. Probert started back and looked at me with something akin to horror. "Not, I pray and trust, named after the unspeakable Oliver Cromwell?"

"Knowing the parent, I would suspect so," interjected Mr. Turnsall.

Mr. Probert fairly pierced me with his small, gimlet-like eyes. "I pity you, boy. Such a name has to be an affliction. How old are you?"

"I am—" I began.

"He is seven!" cut in Mr. Turnsall.

"Seven years old, you say," said Mr. Probert, with a sharp nod. "Very well. We shall enroll him. Thank you, gentlemen. All of Melcombe thanks you. The whole of Great Britain thanks you. King George himself, if he could speak English, would thank you profusely. I say this although I suspect this boy's father would not thank you."

"Just know, boy," Mr. Bicklet said to me, "you will be better cared for here than if you were with your father."

"No doubt about it," agreed Mr. Turnsall.

"We absolutely agree," said Mr. Probert and delivered what might be called a smug simper.

With no further words to me, but after many salutations and bows to Mr. Probert, the two men left. I stood where I was, not sure what was going to happen, but I had no expectations that it would be anything good.

CHAPTER FOURTEEN

A Description of the Children's Poorhouse, and How It Lovingly Cared for Melcombe's Unfortunate Children.

M r. Probert put down his black quill and stared at me with his hard eyes. Once, twice, he adjusted his wig. He jangled his keys.

At length, I fidgeted. That caused him to speak. "The first thing you shall learn, boy, upon entering this institution is that you must remain still. Very still. Learn to stand as straight as a pin. No moving. None."

"I'm sorry, sir, but—"

"And no speaking," he fairly hissed, "unless you are bidden to. You read your Bible, I presume. I sincerely hope you do. Proverbs 21:23. 'Whoso keepeth his mouth and his tongue keepeth his soul from troubles.'"

He patted his wig.

"Furthermore, I want no child enrolled here to have the appalling name of Oliver Cromwell. Rather, we shall call you Charles, after the beloved martyred king who had his head detached so cruelly from his scared body by that tyrant whose name with which you have been branded.

"Now, Charles," he said, "you must cease fidgeting. A restless body reveals a restless soul. Stand straight as a pin. Master that task. Think pin. Be pin." He bent over his book, picked up his quill, and scratched away.

If an itch had a sound, it would have been exactly that noise. At the same time his keys dangled over the edge of his desk, occasionally clicking like an apprehensive cricket.

After a long while, Mr. Probert looked up, patted his wig, and said, "Do you have any idea what I am doing?"

"You are writing, sir."

He nodded. "The poorhouse accounts. It costs eighteen pence per week to maintain and teach each child in this establishment. We have, including you, forty-eight children under our generous care." The keys clinked. "Did you know that?"

"No, sir."

"Children are expensive out of all proportion to their size. Nothing annoys ratepayers as do children. They are the locusts in Deuteronomy 28:38: 'Thou shall carry much seed out into the field, and shall gather but little in; for the locust shall consume it.'

"That is why every child enrolled here works for what they receive. I trust you also know Proverbs 19:15. 'Slothfulness casteth into a deep sleep; and an idle soul shall suffer hunger.' I promise you that we shall endeavor to keep you from being slothful. An authority has written: 'The sooner poor children are put to laborious, painful work the more patiently they will submit to it forever.' Wise words."

Mr. Probert adjusted his wig anew, bent over his desk, and went back to his pen-scratching. I remained standing, listening to his irritating pen.

Time passed. Mr. Probert ignored me. He patted his wig. His keys clicked. At one point, because of an itch, I reached to rub my ear. Without looking up he said, "No fidgeting, Charles. Every time you do so, I shall add ten minutes to your standing. Ten whole minutes. You may rely on that. Think . . . pin." He turned his hourglass over so that the white sand trickled down in a slow, scraggy stream.

I stood there for at least an hour, my time punctuated by his "No fidgeting!" commands, resulting in his turning over the hourglass at least six times. That did not keep him from now and again touching and adjusting his wig.

At one point Mr. Probert said, "I suppose I should inform you, Charles, of our schedule. In summer, we rise at six. In winter, seven. Work commences at eight. Concludes at five. We retire during winter at seven, summer at eight. Breakfast at eight. Dinner at twelve. Supper at six. Chapel at rising. Chapel before bed. Can you read and write?"

"Yes, sir."

"Then you need not attend school lessons, but work more so as to contribute to your generous maintenance."

As I stood there, it occurred to me that I could, if I wanted, turn about and bolt through the main door. I suspect Mr. Probert had the same thought at the very same time, because he abruptly climbed down from behind his desk, key ring in hand. I could hear him (for I dared not turn and look) scuttle down the hallway and then I heard what sounded like the locking of a door.

In other words, I was trapped.

CHAPTER FIFTEEN

The Poorhouse and How It Strove to Make Me, Among Other Children, a Better Person.

I need to tell you about the poorhouse.

On the second, highest floor, on one side, there was an apartment for Mr. Probert. In my time there I never saw it. I asked the other children; no one had ever seen it.

On that same floor, on the other side, was a room, which served as a schoolroom and chapel. There was a pulpit-like podium up front, over which, upon the wall, was written this biblical quotation:

PROVERBS 16:29.
A violent man enticeth his neighbor,
and leadeth him into the way that is not good.

Otherwise, the room had nothing but low benches.

On the main floor were two large rooms, left and right.

The largest was where the poorhouse children did their work. There were some windows, but they were always shut. Meals—breakfast, dinner, and supper—were also served there.

The second room on the first floor was divided in two: half the dormitory for girls, half for boys. The beds were laid out one after the other, with a narrow space between them and an alley along the feet of the beds. The children slept two in a bed, like dead fish in a box.

There was a fireplace, but no fire.

The privy was in the back yard.

The kitchen was in the basement.

Walls were painted a uniform fog-like gray.

Floors of plain wood.

No color anywhere.

No decoration anywhere.

That was the Melcombe Regis Children's Parish Poorhouse.

After standing before Mr. Probert for at least an hour he climbed down from behind his desk, patted his wig, and said, "Come along with me, Charles."

I followed him down the hall, and using a key from his key ring he unlocked the door and we entered the workroom. Some forty-seven children were there, the room divided between girls and boys. They were sitting on long, low benches, hunched over like old people. No one was talking. Perhaps the reason for the silence was due to what was written on the forward wall:

PROVERBS 17:28
Even a fool, when he holdeth his peace, is counted wise:
And he that shutteth his lips is esteemed a man of understanding.

Some of the children were quite young, hardly more than three. None, I thought, was as old as I. Boys and girls were dressed in identical gray smocks, though some were more patched than others. I wondered if their souls were patched.

To one side was a small fireplace, in which I observed two glowing coals, like eyes, half-asleep. They offered little heat.

Suspended from the ceiling, high over the children, was an enormous egg-shaped basket made of rope. Closed off, top and bottom, it was held up by a thick cord, which, by a system of pulleys, extended from the ceiling to a side-wall, down that wall, and tied to a peg. Since it was empty, I had no idea what purpose the basket served.

In front of the room—beneath the written biblical verse—was a boy sitting on a high stool facing the children. In one hand he held the handle of a brass bell. His other hand had a large pocket watch. He appeared to be about ten years old, older than the children before him. Nor did he look as pale or frail as the others.

Before each child was a block of wood on which lay a small iron hammer. On the blocks were what seemed to be two-foot lengths of something black. Some of the children were hitting these things with the hammers, even as others were picking at them. Underneath the benches were reed baskets. Around the children's feet lay small black bits.

When Mr. Probert and I came in, no one looked around but continued what they were doing.

Mr. Probert clapped his hands. "Attention please!"

The children stopped their work and peered round.

"Is everything well, George?" Mr. Probert said to the boy who was sitting up front.

"Yes, sir, Mr. Probert." This boy, I realized, functioned as an overseer.

"Here, children," said Mr. Probert, "is a new boy." He pushed me forward. "He goes by the name of Charles. His wicked father abandoned him. Happily, by the goodness of Mr. Turnsall and Mr. Bicklet, our devoted patrons, he has been rescued."

The children stared at me with faces that could have been chopped from the white cliffs of Dover.

Mr. Probert went on: "While it might be thought that to be abandoned by a father is a bad thing, as many of us know, it is a good thing. His father is—or was; we are not sure if he lives—an evil man, who did sinful things. Charles is fortunate to be here. We intend to make him better than his father."

No one said a word in response.

Mr. Probert looked around. "John," he said. "You may stand."

A boy stood up from the bench upon which he had been sitting. I supposed him to be not more than five years of age, though he was stooped like an old man. His hair was whitish, his face like cold oatmeal and gave no clue about what he was thinking, if anything. His gray smock made me think of him as a beginner ghost though his fingertips were black, as if he had only begun to be dipped into Hell.

"John, you may instruct Charles how we pick oakum, and thereby defray the cost of our town's considerable kindness."

"Yes, sir."

Mr. Probert said, "Charles"—he meant me—"you may sit next to John. George, John has my permission to talk to the new boy."

"Yes, sir, Mr. Probert."

"The rest of you may continue your work," said Mr. Probert, and with that, he patted his wig and headed for the door.

The moment he moved, George, the boy up front, rang his bell. The children resumed their work.

From behind, I heard the sound of a door lock snapping shut.

CHAPTER SIXTEEN

In Which I Am Taught a Useful Occupation.

The boy named John had been sitting close to another boy. That boy squirmed off a little to one side to make some room for me on the bench. I went forward, squeezed in, and sat down.

John did not greet me or introduce himself. He simply said, "Here is what we do."

From the block of wood that was before him, he picked up a black thing, which I now realized was a piece of ship's rope. It had been, as was common for ship rope, coated in tar so as to keep it waterproof.

John took this length of black rope and laid it on the block. Holding his hammer with two hands, he struck the rope length with a smart rap. The tar, no doubt old and stiff, cracked in many places. John now took up the rope piece in his hands and began to pick at the cracked tar.

Small bits dropped to the floor. In the process, John's fingertips turned darker.

Once John had peeled away the tar, which took a while, he began to shred the rope, pulling apart its small fibers. These small, thin threads he deposited with care into the basket under his bench.

While he demonstrated this, John said not a word. Only when he had thoroughly picked apart the rope did he turn to me and say, "That is what we do."

"What are the fibers for?" I asked.

He shrugged listlessly. "It's our work."

(I would learn later that these fiber bits were oakum, about which Mr. Probert had spoken. It was used for caulking between ship planks, rendering boats leak-proof. In a busy port like Melcombe Regis–Weymouth, there was a ready market for it.)

Then, with a nervous glance at George—the boy at the head of the room—John added, "You need to start. We are not meant to be idle." He handed me a length of rope. "You may share my hammer," he said.

I took the rope and did what I had seen John do. At first it did not seem hard. But very quickly it grew tedious. My fingers began to ache, even as they turned black with the tar.

I don't know how long I had worked when George rang his bell. There was a general rustle in the room. The children put down their work and sat up. There was even some quiet chatter among them. Five girls stood and left the room. I looked to John for an explanation.

"The girls will be bringing dinner," he said.

That pleased me, for I was famished. "Is the food good?" I asked.

"Today we have oatmeal pudding," he said and then added, "with a pat of butter."

For the first time the boy on my other side spoke. "Tomorrow's dinner is milk porridge."

"Sunday," said the boy in front of me, "we have beef, pudding, and broth." He spoke with little energy.

"What is for supper?" I asked.

"Today we'll have bread and butter."

"Tomorrow bread and cheese."

"And breakfast?"

"Hasty pudding."

"Or milk porridge."

"Sometimes beef broth."

The girls who had left the room returned with wooden bowls and spoons, the bowls half filled with the pudding. They distributed all they had, then left to return with more, until every child had a bowl. George, the boy at the head of the class, had two bowls. No one ate until all had bowls.

Ravenous, I consumed my pudding in moments. Others

ate more slowly as if not wanting to reach the bottoms of their bowls too soon.

The bell was rung again. The bowls were collected, the work on the ropes resumed for the rest of the afternoon. No one spoke or left their benches.

As the hours went by my fingers ached badly. I was bored beyond belief. My plan had been to stay at the poorhouse for two weeks or until such time as my father returned. But as I sat there, I told myself I could not, would not stay that long. I had to get out. The sooner the better.

CHAPTER SEVENTEEN

My Time in the Poorhouse, During Which I Grew Rich with Experience.

I spent the rest of the day picking oakum, monotonous beyond belief. My fingers became numb and black. My arms and back ached. Any number of times, I had to stop working, sit up and stretch. Each time I did, George, the boy at the head of the class, called, "You! New boy! Learn the rules! No idleness! Keep on!"

I loathed him.

Work did not cease until five o'clock, at which time the bell was rung. The black bits were swept up. For supper, as promised, bread with butter was served. The bread was cut to a one-inch thickness, but the butter was very thin. I had to tilt the slice to see its sheen.

During our bread and butter dinner the boys and girls were again separated. I sat with John.

"How long have you been here?" I asked, keeping my voice low. I had already learned that to speak loudly was an offence.

John looked at me as if he had never been asked that question. After a moment, he whispered, "I don't know."

"No idea?"

He shook his head.

"How old are you?"

Once again he shook his head.

I turned to the boy on my other side. "What's your name?"

"Richard."

"Richard what?"

He shrugged.

"How long have you been here?"

He seemed to think, only to say, "A long time."

Once dinner was done—I was still hungry—we were led to the chapel by the same monitor, the boy called George.

Mr. Probert was waiting for us, standing behind the podium when we entered. We sat on benches, boys on one side, girls on the other. I noticed Mr. Probert had brought his hourglass, which he rested by his side and in sight of us all. As always, he clutched his keys, and was continually caressing his wig.

He began by saying, "There will be no fidgeting during

chapel. I will call out anyone who even twiddles. I trust I am being understood by you, Charles."

None of the children said anything. They just sat there. Mr. Probert began to speak. His talk was about how lucky we children were to be in the poorhouse, learning a trade, how to read, being well housed and fed. "If you weren't here, you—abandoned by your wicked fathers and mothers—would be dead," he proclaimed.

In the middle of his sermon he suddenly called out, "Mary!" He pointed. "Stand up!"

It was the same little girl who had opened the front door.

"Mary, I would have thought after two years here you would have learned that you must remain still. Very still. Now, stand as straight as a pin. No moving. None. Pin!" With those words Mr. Probert turned his hourglass so that the white sand began to slither slowly down.

Mary stood quite still, though I could see her small fingers twitch behind her back.

Chapel over, we washed our faces in a great pot of cold water that stood next to the privy. As for the privy, we were lined up and allowed to use it in turn.

Afterward we were marched to our bed area. I was paired with John, the two of us in a narrow bed; we slept on thin flock mattresses. Over us was a thin blanket.

The candle was capped. It became dark.

For the first time John asked me a question. He spoke in an undertone: "Did your father truly abandon you?"

"Not really," I said. "He'll be back soon."

"Everybody says that," he said. "What happened to your mother?"

"She died when I was born."

"A lot of children say that, too."

"What happened to your parents?" I asked.

"I don't know."

"Do you ever think of running away?" I asked John.

He thought a moment and then said, "Where would I go?"

"Does no one object to the work?"

"If you do, the punishment is terrible," he said.

George must have had his bell, because it rang, so that John rolled away, making it clear he did not wish to talk anymore.

I lay under the cover and rubbed my hands, one against the other. They ached.

After a while I could tell by John's steady breath that he had fallen asleep. I sat up. Moonlight came through the windows, enough so I could see no movement in the room. I was fairly sure that all the boys in the room slept.

As I lay there I made up my mind to run away, go home, fetch the money, and take the early stagecoach to London. Even so, I remained perfectly still wanting to make sure no one was awake. Now and again one of the boys twitched but it was to no account.

Sure I would not be discovered, I swung my legs out from the blanket and stood up on the cold floor. Moving quietly, I walked down the aisle between the bed rows and tried the dormitory door. It was open. I stepped from the room into the main hallway, where the moonlight allowed me to make my way.

I crept down the hallway until I reached the front door. Grasping the door handle I pulled. It was locked.

Frustrated, but more determined than ever, I went into the workroom and attempted to open one of the windows. It would not budge. I tried another window. It too would not move. I didn't bother with the other windows, assuming that they were also shut. Finally I made my way to the back door, which led to the privy. It was locked.

I now understood why Mr. Probert carried his keys about. The poorhouse was little more than a prison.

Disheartened, I made my way back to the boys' sleeping room and returned to bed. As I lay there I had a new and disturbing thought: I had left no message as to my whereabouts at home. When my father returned, if he returned, how would he know where I was?

CHAPTER EIGHTEEN

During Which, Following Mr. Probert's Educational Principles, I Rise High.

Winter may not have truly come, but it was brittle cold the next morning when we were summoned at six a.m. by the sound of a ringing bell. Half-asleep, yawning, stumbling, rubbing faces, a long shivery line was made for the outside privy. In the workroom we had a breakfast of hasty pudding—bread crumbs with some wheat flour and a little butter, cooked in milk until it becomes a slushy batter.

Breakfast consumed, we took our places in the upstairs chapel and heard a brief sermon from Mr. Probert, interrupted by his constant adjustments to his wig.

For his text he used Philippians 2:14–15: "Do all things without grumbling or disputing that you may be blameless and innocent." His eyes were fastened upon me.

We marched back into the workroom. The door was locked behind us. George directed me to my own place and I was provided with my own wood block, hammer, and basket for fibers. Once all were in place the bell rang and we commenced picking oakum. There was little noise save for the continual *tat-tat-tat* of hammers, and the sound of small fingers plucking at the tar, like the scurrying of mice in walls.

George was perched upon his stool up front—reminding me of a gargoyle—bell in one hand, large watch in his other. Now and again he would call out such things as, "William! No fidgeting!" Or, "Charlotte! Attend to your work!" At one point he addressed his remarks to me: "Charles! Do not look at me!"

I worked, trying to keep to my task. It took no thought whatsoever. Picking at the rope was drearisome beyond belief, repetitious, and painful to my hands, whose fingertips again turned black with tar. After a while I fell into a stupor, so that my thoughts were the color of the walls—gray.

The bell rang for lunch. Lunch consisted of a bowl of three baked ox cheeks. Gritty. Tough. Awful.

The door was unlocked and we were offered privy time. Then a return to work, the door locked. The bell rang and we started to work again.

I don't know how long I picked at the oakum—perhaps

97

for as long as two hours beyond lunch. All the while I felt a growing rage until at last I threw down the hammer and cried out, "This is completely . . . stupid!"

As I told you, the children in the room worked in near silence. When I cried out as I did, all work stopped. The silence grew yet deeper, as if emptiness could empty into something even less than vacant. The children, open-mouthed, swiveled round to stare at me, making it clear something unique had happened.

"Charles!" cried George from the front of the room. "Did you call out?"

"My name is not Charles!" I returned. "It is Oliver! Oliver Cromwell Pitts. And I said this work is stupid! S. T. U. P. I. D. Dead-hearted! I won't do it anymore!"

"You are not allowed to say that," returned George. "You're a homeless child. You are obliged to do as you're told."

"It's boring! Pointless!"

"Richard!" cried George. "Fetch Mr. Probert!"

The boy named Richard jumped up and ran to the door, and tried to open it. "It's locked," he said, his voice full of dread.

"Here," said George. "The key!" He held one up.

Richard raced back, took the key, and hurried to the door.

"Lock the door when you go out," cautioned George.

I heard him unlock the door, step out. I also heard the sound of clacking as the lock closed.

Knowing that Mr. Probert was about to come, the children swung back around, bent over their wood blocks, and began to work harder than ever, hammers tripping as fast as bird hearts. The tension in the room was such that I was sure I could hear it like a vibrating string.

"Charles," cried George. He was pleading. "You need to resume your work."

"I won't do it anymore."

"Do you know what will happen to you?" said George, looking truly frightened. I will credit him; he was warning me.

"I don't care," I returned.

"You will," he said. "I'm giving you a last chance. Go back to work!"

"No!"

Behind me I heard the sound of the door lock opening. All work in the room stopped. The silence was profound. Trembling, I kept my eyes forward.

The door lock shut with a snap.

Mr. Probert's voice commenced, cold, slow, and raspy: "What . . . is . . . going . . . on . . . here?"

George, breathless, said, "It's . . . the new boy, sir.

Charles. He . . . he won't work. He says it's . . . stu . . . stupid." Speaking the last word, his voice faltered, as if its use was particularly prohibited.

Mr. Probert advanced to the front of the room. For a moment he simply stood there. His only movement was to touch his wig. In one hand was a large padlock. His sharp eyes were fixed on me.

"Charles," he said. "You . . . may . . . stand."

I stood.

"Did you say the work was . . .'stupid'?"

"Yes, sir. And . . . and pointless."

Mr. Probert remained still, as if he found it difficult to grasp the full weight of my words.

Then he said, "You are here, Charles, as an act of kindness bestowed upon you by the generous ratepayers of Melcombe Regis. Your feeble mother died giving you life. Your valueless father left you homeless. Starving. He abandoned you. You are here as an act of charity."

"My father did not abandon me!" I shouted.

"Well then, where is he? Why does he not come and fetch you? Does he not want you? No, he does not want you. You are here because no one wants you."

Ashamed, I stood there, trying to squeeze back the tears welling in my eyes.

"Do you know what happens to those who will not

work?" said Mr. Probert. "Who speak violence?" He pointed to the Proverb on the wall.

"No, sir."

"I shall show you. George, Richard, lower the basket."

The boys hurried to the side of the room.

As I have informed you, suspended from the ceiling was a huge net-like basket woven out of rope.

The boys untied the cord holding it in place and lowered the basket. Even as I watched, I still did not understand what it was. But as the basket came to the ground the children immediately beneath it scurried away. They seemed to know exactly what was happening.

"James! Henry! William! Edward!" cried Mr. Probert. "Take hold of Charles."

(Only later did it occur to me that Mr. Probert had renamed all the boys after English kings.)

Four boys sprang up, and before I understood what was being done, came round and grabbed my arms, and though I tried to resist, there were too many arms holding me.

"Put him in!" cried Mr. Probert.

The four fairly flung me into the huge basket.

Then Mr. Probert drew two strands of the rope together and padlocked them. As I became entangled in the rope, the boys rushed back to the wall and began to haul on the cord. The basket went up. I tried to get out, but aside from the fact that the opening was padlocked, my feet kept slipping through the gaps in the rope, effectively entrapping me. What's more, even as the basket was hauled high into the air, the rope weave closed round me.

The cord holding the basket was then tied to a wall peg by some of the boys. All of which meant I was suspended high in the air in what truly was a cage of rope.

"Very well, Charles," Mr. Probert called up to me. "You will remain there for twenty-four hours. While you are there, I urge you to think about the charity that has been bestowed upon you. I trust when you come down, if you are allowed to come down, you will be ready to resume working. But only if you don't speak such violence."

That said, he turned to the gawking children, adjusted his wig, and said, "It is Charles who has behaved badly, but it should be a lesson for all of you. Now, back to work."

George clanged his dulsome bell.

Below me, the now silent children bent over their oakum picking. As for me, I hung above them, hardly knowing what to do.

What I did know is that I had been sentenced to remain there until the next day—unless I could escape.

CHAPTER NINETEEN

In Which I Tell You of My Time in the Basket.

Living by the sea as I did, I had seen many a fish caught in a net; saw them flop about as they were drawn up, gasping for breath, altogether helpless. I admit I never bestowed much sympathy upon any fish. Now it was me who was caught.

I tried to get out, but the weave of the basket was such that one, I could get no firm footing, and two, when I pushed against the ropes in one direction, another part of the basket closed round me. Moreover, there was that padlock, which prevented me from pulling the entryway open; a cage that measured itself to me.

I did call out "Let me down! Let me out!" any number of times. Not one of the children below me budged. A few glanced up, displaying affrightment on their faces—

perhaps some sympathy—but they were hastily scolded into submission by George clanging his bell.

I found it exhausting to try and stand erect. Though I attempted to hold myself up, I kept slipping through the net holes.

It didn't take long before I became weary, stopped struggling, and simply lay back, which was the most comfortable position. But that was the position of acceptance. The posture filled me with a sense of failure; it was as if I was giving up.

Below me, the life of the poorhouse resumed in shockingly ordinary fashion. *Tat-tat-tat* went the hammers. *Pluck-pick-pluck-pick* went the children's fingers. No one spoke. As far as I could tell, I was barely noticed. Yet I had the sensation that everyone knew where I was.

Is there anything more terrifying than the silence that knows of awfulness but speaks it not?

At what must have been five o'clock George rang the bell. The children below ceased their work, swept up, and filed obediently out of the room. I think I saw John steal a look up at me, the briefest of glances. It was as if he was too affrightened to do even that much.

I heard the door shut. Heard it lock. Was I to be left? I could not believe it.

Yes, I was left.

It grew dark. Utterly soundless. Cold, too. When I

moved, the basket swung gently, rather like the pendulum of a ceaselessly ticking clock at which no one looks.

For me time seemed to stop.

I spent the entire night hanging there. To be sure I became horribly hungry, shivered mightily, and tried to recall what was being eaten for supper. I could not. Now and again I struggled. At one point I had the notion that if I swung the basket wildly, it might break and fall. The fear of falling, crashing down, seemed small compared to possible freedom.

By throwing myself this way and that I did get the basket to swing in wild, twisting arcs, but nothing happened—in regard to my freedom—except that I grew nauseous.

At length I ceased the swaying and remembered my father's letter, which I had put in my pocket. I pulled it out and studied it. There was just enough moonlight to let me read. Once again I tried to guess the meaning of "mXXXXXd!!" Had my sister been mistreated? Misunderstood? Clearly something dreadful must have happened to draw my father so. But there I was, incapable of helping.

The more I thought and fretted about it the more I realized I should not wait for Father's return. Aside from hating the way I had been treated, I was angry at my father for all the enemies he had made, foes who were pleased to make life miserable for me.

Very well, I would leave Melcombe and never return. I would go to London. Charity had promised she would take me in. I had to find her.

Yet it must be said that too often people make the most ambitious plans when they are least capable of achieving them. A small, sensible desire is a large fantasy if it cannot be achieved. I was no exception. In my head I climbed mountains. In reality I could barely move. Instead I lay there, until I grew all too aware that I needed to use the privy. "Let me down!" I began to shout. "For a moment! I promise I'll come back! I need the privy!" I screamed.

No one came. I wet myself, and felt nothing but shame.

Punish a child and he will be angry. Humiliate a child and he will remember forever.

The night wore on. I thought about that storm. Oh, how it had already changed my life.

At some point I slept. Not soundly. Or well. But sleep I did, dreaming of being trapped forever. Alas, it was no dream.

CHAPTER TWENTY

A Short Chapter on a Lengthy Subject.

Dawn came, bringing some little light to the room. I remained where I was, on my back, in the net, damp, smelling badly, mortified, wondering if I would truly be kept in the basket for the full twenty-four hours.

As if from a great distance I heard the bell ring, then the children moving about. I dozed. The sound of the door unlocking woke me. With George leading, the boys and girls filed into the room and took their stations. None looked up at me, but a few wrinkled their noses, so I knew they smelled me.

Once the door was locked George rang the bell, and the children sat down and commenced their oakum plucking. Shortly after, Mr. Probert came in.

"I hope you are learning your lesson, Charles," he called out.

If ever I hated anyone in my life it was Mr. Probert.

"That, children," he announced, pointing up, "will be your fate if you do not follow the rules. If you speak violently. Your task is to humbly learn to work. You may carry on."

Locking the door behind him, he left the room. I began plotting, imagining terrible revenge on the man. My father had spoken of public executions in London. I fantasized how I might bring them to Melcombe. Mr. Probert had said my namesake, Oliver Cromwell, took off a king's head. I contemplated every cruelty upon the schoolmaster, with a decided emphasis on head removal.

The day wore on with excruciating slowness. Thirst. Hunger. Stiffness. Yet there I was, hanging in the basket, incapable of going anywhere. Waiting. Waiting. Waiting. Waiting to leave Melcombe Regis.

Except, I could not.

CHAPTER TWENTY-ONE

In Which I Continue My Time in the Basket and What Happened.

I squirmed, fidgeted, and ached as I tried, vainly, to find a position of comfort. Below me, the children were fed their lunch, thin pea soup, I believe. Even though I was sure it tasted buggish, my stomach groaned with hunger.

The afternoon commenced. I continued where I was, hanging there like a solitary, rotten apple on a neglected tree.

At some point in time—I was in a kind of stupor—I heard the door unlock. I looked down. Mr. Probert entered the room. He walked forward with the slow measure of a majestic monarch. As far as I could tell, he did not look at me, not until he reached the front of the class.

Once there, he patted his wig and clasped his hands.

"Dear children," he began, "it always gives me pain,

more pain than you experience, when I have to punish you. But the sooner, and more completely, you learn obedience, the happier your life will become. Your duty is to obey. Never let the word 'boring' come to your lips. To complain is to be violent and violence is unlawful. As for what is and is not 'stupid,' children do not have the intelligence to judge anything. Let your elders teach you what is stupid. Let this boy"—he pointed to me—"be an example to you when you behave badly.

"Now, Charles has been there twenty-four hours. It is his own fault. His weakness. I shall now, with great kindness, release him in the hope he has learned his lesson."

With that, he called upon the same boys he had used before—the kings James, Henry, William, and Edward—and told them to lower me. "Do so gently," he said grandly. He also added, "Out of the kindness of my heart I shall help Charles out of the basket."

The four boys got up and went to where the cord was tied to the wall. Below me, the children scrambled away, providing an open space for my return to earth. Mr. Probert moved in place, the better to receive me.

Down I came, inch by inch, but even as I dropped, my anger rose.

I hauled myself into some kind of standing position. When I touched the ground, Mr. Probert stepped forward and unlocked the padlock that kept me entrapped.

Leaving the sprung lock in place, he pulled the ropes apart and reached in to help me step free.

I should be very proud of myself if I told you that what occurred next was something I had planned. Not so. Despite my fury and desire for revenge, I was as surprised as everyone else in the room as to what happened.

As Mr. Probert, in an awkward, bent position, reached in with his hand, I leaned forward and snatched his wig—that crown of smug authority—plucked it right off his head, and flung it behind me into the basket-net. This revealed that his natural hair was an astonishing red color.

Mr. Probert—I am sure it was his vanity—forgot about me and lunged for his precious wig. At that moment, I burst past him, turned about, and using two hands, shoved him into the net. He fell forward, tried to find his footing, but instantly became entangled in the ropes the way I had become.

Quickly, I took hold of the padlock and snapped it shut, so that the entryway was closed tight, Mr. Probert within.

Free of the net, I shouted, "Pull him up!"

It has always been a wonder to me that the four boys—perhaps because they were so used to doing exactly what they were told—did what I called upon them to do.

They hauled up the cord.

As they did, Mr. Probert rose up into the air, even

as he flailed about. As he tried to fix his wig back on his head with one hand and open the net with the other, he dropped his keys, all the while shouting, "Let me out, you miserable mumpers! Let me down!"

"Higher!" I shouted and the boys pulled harder. Then I rushed to where they stood holding the cord, and tied it round the peg, so that Mr. Probert remained hanging high in the air in his own net.

More astonishing than all of that was the reaction of the children. Once Mr. Probert was in the air, locked in, they began to jump up and down, all the while shrieking and squealing in high, youthful voices, "He's caught! He's caught! Hurrah! Hurrah!" Nothing less than joyful pandemonium filled the room.

Meanwhile, George, at the front of the room, was wildly ringing his bell, but no one was paying any attention to him.

I cannot tell you the name of the child who picked up Mr. Probert's keys. All I know is that she held them triumphantly over her head, while shouting, "The keys!"

Then she ran to the door and unlocked it. The children, yelling and shouting with thrilling excitement, poured out of the room, down the hall, me in their midst. The girl with the keys unlocked the front door and, grinning broadly, stepped aside, allowing me to burst out of the poorhouse to my freedom, the children's shouts of encouragement filling my ears.

I expected the children would escape with me. They did not. Later, upon much sad reflection, I realized they had no place to go. This is to say, unlike me, they had no home which to return. But I had, and home is where I headed, as fast as I could go, utterly intent upon fleeing from Melcombe!

I galloped past the customs house and was fast approaching the guild hall when to my horror, I saw Mr. Bartholomew step out of the building. He was with another man, no one I recognized.

I halted instantly and made a quick detour round the corner of St. Mary's Street, then edged forward and peeked. The fellow the customs master was talking to was a young man in a stylish green jacket with buttons from neck to hem, plus fine lace at his wide cuffs. Black riding boots came above his knees. He also had a fine tricorn hat, a plumey white feather attached. He seemed to be an elegant gentleman.

The two men were in close conversation, Mr. Bartholomew doing most of the talking. At one point the customs master extended his hand, as if measuring height. They might even have been measuring my height.

Quite suddenly, the young man glanced up, perhaps

seeing me, and walked off. The next moment Mr. Bicklet and Mr. Turnsall emerged from the guild hall suggesting that it was their arrival that caused the young man's abrupt departure. It was bad enough to see the duo who had locked me up in a children's prison. I was reminded that in the basement of the guild hall was the town gaol. After a brief, animated conversation, the three men, Messrs. Bartholomew, Turnsall, and Bicklet—my enemies as sure as they were my father's—began to walk in the direction of the children's poorhouse.

To be sure, I did not know for certain where they were going, but if their destination was the poorhouse, I knew only too well what they would discover. Once they did, I had no doubt that they would come straight to my home in search of me.

I had to get there before them, change out of my foul-smelling clothing, and retrieve the hidden money. I knew, too, precisely where to go next: the Bear Inn where I would catch the next flying stage to London.

CHAPTER TWENTY-TWO

In Which I Return Home Only to Be Surprised.

I was more than happy to see my home. I was, however, not happy to see our neighbor, Mr. Tickmorton, working before his house, using a straw broom to sweep away the last storm debris from before his door.

Living alone, Mr. Tickmorton was always—save the morning of the storm—wanting to talk to us, being inquisitive about our lives, forever asking about our comings and goings. Though another of my father's enemies, he had never been anything but kind to me so I had no reason to rebuff him. Still, I had no desire to pause and converse, and would have gone right by, but he called out, "Master Oliver! A good day to you, boy. A word with you, please."

Common politeness required me to halt.

"Forgive me for not talking to you the other morning. I

was much troubled. But now I have learned," he said, "that your father has gone away, to London."

"Yes, sir, on business," I said, not wishing to share more information with the man. But as ever, I put on my smile.

"Lawyer business?" Mr. Tickmorton persisted in his prying way.

"He didn't tell me, sir, but I suppose so."

"Will he be back soon?"

"As soon as he can, sir, I'm sure."

"No one was in your home last night," he announced. "Where were you?" It was as if he had some right to know.

"Please, sir," I said. "I've been to the other side of town. With friends."

"Will you be cleaning up the jumble before your house?" he asked, gesturing to the pile of bricks that had been our chimney.

"Presently, sir," I said, wanting only to get into my house, so I could escape town.

No sooner did I take a step in the direction of our door than Mr. Tickmorton announced, "I need to tell you that a short while ago a man was inquiring for you."

That stopped me. "Who was it?"

"The customs master, Mr. Bartholomew. He's the one that told me your father had gone to London. He also told me about a wreck along the beach. He actually had one of the crew with him. Something about a missing

116

twenty-three shillings. I thought it was your father he wished to speak to. A legal affair. But no, it was you he needed to see. Do you know something about those shillings?"

I was stunned. Mr. Bartholomew had brought a sailor from *The Rose in June* to my door. Were the shillings I took his? How else could Mr. Bartholomew know the sum? At the time I took the money I told myself it belonged to a perished sailor. Now he had come to my door. His being alive meant I was a thief.

"Excuse me, sir," I said. "I must go."

"Mr. Bartholomew said he would return."

That stopped me yet again. "He did?"

"Indeed," said Mr. Tickmorton, and the way he looked at me suggested he was eager for more information.

"Excuse me, sir. I must go!" With that I fled into the house and ran up the steps to my room at the top of the house. There I opened the chest that contained my small stock of clothing. I took what I needed. Then I tore down to the back of the house where we had a barrel full of rainwater. I stripped off my old, malodorous outfit and washed my body, face, and fingers. Once clean—the fingers only partly—I dressed in dry linen and clothing. Feeling the better for it, I returned to the house.

Very hungry—I had not eaten in twenty-four hours; what people called having a wolf in my stomach—I searched diligently for some food knowing I had no idea when I'd eat again. By good chance I found an old piece of cheese on a shelf in my father's room. I devoured it on the spot. Though it churned my belly it helped to dampen my hunger.

I cast an eye about to make sure I had whatever might prove useful. With winter approaching, I decided to take my father's heavy coat. A hat, too, one with a fine velvet band round the crown. Though both were too big for me, I remembered how cold I'd been the night before inside the poorhouse and thought it best to prepare for November nights on my way to London.

Finally, I approached the fireplace, stripped off my father's coat and hat, stepped into the hearth, and began to climb. I was in such a hurry I didn't bother with a candle. In any case, with our chimney gone, there was enough light coming down the shaft to show me the way.

It was not hard to see the place where I had set the coins, and was just about to reach for them when I heard Mr. Tickmorton's voice: "If you please, gentlemen, I just saw the boy go into the house. I'm certain he's there. Please go in. He's sure to welcome you and answer all your questions."

"We shall do exactly that," said a slow, raspy voice that I instantly recognized as belonging to Mr. Probert. "Mr. Bartholomew, Mr. Bicklet, Mr. Turnsall, please, you sirs. Do enter."

CHAPTER TWENTY-THREE

What I Learned While in the Chimney.

I dared not move from my place in the chimney but remained where I was, holding myself up by spreading my feet wide and standing on the brick edges.

"What a disgraceful mess," said a voice I recognized as belonging to Mr. Bartholomew.

"What one might expect from such people." That was Mr. Turnsall.

"Charles!" shouted Mr. Probert. "You must surrender to us immediately!"

"I shall fetch him," said Mr. Bicklet.

Thinking they knew where I had hidden, I was terrified.

Next moment I heard the tread of someone walking up the steps. They believed I was in the upper part of the house.

"Are you going to arrest him immediately?" came Mr. Turnsall's voice.

"It's my duty," said Mr. Bartholomew. "I have no doubt he's a thief. I've already arranged that the guild hall gaol be ready."

"Is it a hanging offence?" asked Mr. Probert with some delight, I thought.

"Twenty-three shillings!" said Mr. Bartholomew. "I should say so."

"I wish to lay a charge against the boy, too," said Mr. Probert. "Can you imagine, without cause, he assaulted me."

"Let him hang then, twice," said Mr. Bartholomew. "I've been called to London this week. Crown customs matters. I shall make it my business to secure a general warrant against the boy. One way or another, gentlemen, I intend to be done with him. And by linking him to his father, we can have that unpleasant man transported out of the kingdom entirely."

I heard the sound of someone coming down the steps. Mr. Bicklet's voice: "He's not here."

"Cunning thief!" exclaimed Mr. Bartholomew. "Just like his father. I'll wager the boy's trying to get to London to join him."

"Gentlemen," said Mr. Turnsall. "I propose we inform Mr. Webber at the Bear Inn about the boy so as to stop him from getting on the London coach. Confine him to

120

Melcombe and Melcombe's gaol. Keeping him might even lure the father back."

Within moments they left.

Though relieved to learn that my original plan to go to the Bear Inn would entrap me, my father's enemies (now mine as well) left me with no way to get to London unless I walked the hundred and twenty-eight miles.

CHAPTER TWENTY-FOUR

In Which I Decide on a Course of Action.

Once I was sure my foes had truly moved on, I gathered the (now) stolen shillings from where I had placed them up the chimney and stuffed them into my trouser pocket. Money secured, I climbed down to the parlor.

It would have been easy to think of my enemies as stupid and incapable. As it turned out, they were clever, whereas it was I who had been stupid.

As I stood there, I realized I had few choices:

One: I could go back to *The Rose in June*, replace the money, and thereby free myself from the charge of being a thief.

But what if I was discovered doing so? I would be arrested, never reach London, and be hanged for my pains.

Second option: I could take the money, go to Mr.

Bartholomew, bend my knee, admit my theft, and beg for forgiveness.

But what if he refused to forgive me, and for my honesty, threw me into gaol and then hanged me?

Third, I could make my escape from town, take to the road, and find my way to London. Once there, I would locate my sister and my father and let them solve all my difficulties.

But what if I could not find them?

I must find them!

Oh, irony: the money I had thought would keep me safe in Melcombe until my father returned was now forcing me to flee Melcombe! Unfortunately, though I had money enough, I could not simply get on the coach and go.

My solution? I would creep out of town and commence walking along the Dorchester Road, which would take me beyond Melcombe Regis. After some miles I'd wait, hail the passing stagecoach, get on, and proceed to London.

I was resolved never to see Melcombe again.

I did consider holding back until night as a way of keeping out of view, but I was too unsettled to wait. Besides it was already late afternoon. There was the real possibility my adversaries might come back and apprehend me. In haste then, I put on my father's winter coat and his hat.

Making sure the money was safe in my pocket, I peeked out the front door. Mr. Tickmorton had placed a stool before his house and was sitting there, commanding a complete view of my movements. No doubt he had been engaged as a lurker by my enemies.

I left the house through the back door, into our yard. Once there, it was a simple matter for me to climb the fence, jump down into the narrow alley, and step onto Maiden Street. Then I headed northeast, running as fast as I could.

CHAPTER TWENTY-FIVE

In Which I Hid and What Came of That.

By the time I started my escape, daylight had diminished. It was also becoming colder, the wind slicing off the bay with considerable sharpness. I was glad I had Father's coat wrapped around me, his hat on my head, and could only hope it would not get colder. Still, I was in need of some protected place, where I could wait unnoticed through the night until the morning when I could hail the passing London stage.

As Melcombe Regis is situated on a peninsula, the adjacent land quickly becomes constricted as you travel northeast. In fact, the way is called "the Narrows." Thus, to my right was the beach and bay. To the left was what we called the Back Sea. The road I was on obliged me to go right by the Bear Inn.

Certain that Mr. Webber—the innkeeper—had already been told to watch for me, I ran for all I was worth, making every effort not to look in the direction of the inn. By not looking where Mr. Webber might be, I thought it might keep him from looking at me. So it is we often look upon our troubles.

In any case, no one hailed me, and I continued on. The farther I got beyond the Bear Inn the more relieved I felt. Happily, though night was fast advancing, a big moon was already high in the sky and lit the way.

As I hurried north, I began to grasp that I had a major dilemma: I did not know when the stage left the inn for London, neither the time of day nor for that matter which day. For all I knew it might be every day, or every other day.

I tried to recall when Charity had gone. I knew she had departed early in the morning, but which day quite escaped me.

As I struggled with this problem, I came upon Mountjoy Fort.

Mountjoy Fort sits northeast of Melcombe Regis, at the slenderest part of the Narrows. It is so situated that its cannon had pointed toward Weymouth Bay as well as northward from which attacks upon Melcombe most likely would have come.

The fort had been important during the last century's civil wars. Since then it had fallen into disuse and it was common knowledge there were neither cannon nor soldiers there. While not a complete ruin, some of the circular walls had tumbled. My friends and I had played there, finding it full of hiding places.

Because it was close to the only road, the Dorchester Road that led from Melcombe Regis to London, I decided it was an excellent place in which to hide, wait, and keep watch for the stagecoach. As soon as the stage showed itself—whenever that might be—I would be in a position to hail it.

The fort's main entryway was right on the road. If there had been a defensive gate, it was long gone, which meant I was able to look right in and out. Moonlight allowed me to observe that its central area was filled with little but mounds of rubble. I'd be able to sit by the entry and have a clear view of the approaching stagecoach.

Then I noticed a small glimmering of light emanating from behind a heap of rocks off to one side. It took a moment for me to realize it was not moonlight. Curious, I went forward, climbed the mound, and peeked over. A man was sitting on the ground before a small fire.

Even as I peeked over the rubble and gazed at him, wondering who and why he was there, I accidentally caused a small stone to tumble down on the other side of the mound. The sound was slight but in an instant, the man turned and leveled a pistol right at me.

CHAPTER TWENTY-SIX

In Which I Engage with the Man with the Pistol.

The man and I stared at each other. I did consider running away, but when I heard the click of the hammer being cocked, and understood the pistol was aimed right at me, I was persuaded to do otherwise. Besides, I was having trouble breathing.

"Who are you?" the man demanded. "Raise your hands quickly, or I'll blow out your brains."

I lifted my trembling hands. "Please, sir. I'm Oliver Pitts."

"Stand up and show yourself."

I did as I was told.

"What are you doing here?"

"I was just . . . passing by."

"Passing by? Here? At this hour? Where do you come from?"

"Melcombe, sir."

"Come down from behind those stones so I can see you better." He motioned with his free hand, but kept his gun aimed at me.

Still keeping my hands up, I managed to get over the rocks, and then stumble down to the man's level, my heart full of fright.

What I could make of him in that disconsolate place beneath the moonlight (and his fire) was that his face was haggard, weary, with wide, wild eyes. Ill-kempt, he wore no wig, but had long, dark, tangled hair that reached his shoulders. He was wearing what appeared to be a dark jacket with dull buttons (some missing) along with bits of tattered lace at the cuffs. One sleeve was torn. Around his neck was a black cloth. His riding boots were patched. All in all, there was something fierce about him, suggesting ragged violence. Moreover, his pistol, leveled at me, seemed to twitch in his hand, so that I feared it would fire all on its own. All the while he studied me as if trying to decide whether or not to shoot me.

"Take off your hat," he commanded.

When I did, his face registered disgust. "You're just a boy!" he exclaimed. "Your hat and coat are too big for you. Did you steal them?"

"No, sir. They belong to my father."

"Running away?"

"Please, sir. I'm on my way to finding him in London."

"Escaping from an apprenticeship then?"

"No, sir. I'm apprenticed to my father."

"What's his trade?"

"Lawyer, sir."

"Lawyers are dogs," he said and spat upon the ground. "How did you intend to get to London?" he asked, not for a moment lowering his pistol.

"I was going to take the stagecoach, sir."

"The stagecoach doesn't stop here."

I said nothing.

"The coach costs money. Do you have some then?"

In a small show of courage, I kept my mouth closed.

"Have you money?" he demanded, and he stretched out his arm so the barrel of his pistol was that much closer to my thumping chest.

When I remained silent, he said, "Don't be a fool! I can as easily take money from a crashed boy as a live one. You won't be the first I'll have slayed. Now then, do you have money?"

His violent speech, along with the elevated pistol, proved a potent persuader. "Yes, sir. I have some."

"Give it over then."

"Please, sir, if I do, I won't be able to get to London."

"You can go to the devil for all I care," he cried. "I need money more than you do!" He extended his free hand—a dirty one—toward me, palm up, while the other hand waggled his pistol ominously.

I reached into my pocket and, choosing to let some coins remain, pulled forth a fistful of shillings. When I held out what I had, the man snatched them.

"Are you sure that's all?" he said. "I'll beat you to a bloody rag if I find more when I search you."

In haste, I took out the remaining shillings and gave them over. He dropped them into his jacket pocket.

"Any more?"

"No, sir. Please, can I go now?"

"And raise a hue and cry against me? I think not. Come here. Be fast! Sit on the other side of the fire so I can see you better." He pointed to the spot with his pistol.

I sat as ordered. When I did, he resumed his place on the far side of the fire opposite me, the pistol still in his grip.

The light of the flames let me see him better. The more I observed him, the more I could see that he was an angersome man. His mouth was twitchy, his face flushed, and his wide eyes were bloodshot. Moreover, the way he kept fluttering his pistol suggested he was still trying to decide whether or not to use it.

"Have any food?" he asked.

"No, sir."

Shivering from dread as much as from the cold, I pulled

my coat tightly around me, squashed my hat down on my head, and leaned forward so I could absorb some of the fire's warmth on my face. Having before never encountered such a violent man, I could not stop quaking.

"Now then," he demanded, "I want no chimney-corner tales. You say you are going to your father."

"It's true, sir."

"Then why are you here—at night?"

"I wanted to hail the stage."

"From here?"

"Yes, sir."

"So as to rob it?"

"To ride it," I pleaded. "I was going to pay my way with that money I gave you."

He studied me. "You said you've come from town and you had money. Why didn't you get on the stage there?"

I stayed mute. In the silence I heard a horse whinny from somewhere in the fort. I turned toward the sound.

"My horse," he said. "Keep your eyes on me." After a moment he said, "Do you know who I am? Why I am here?"

His looks, way of acting, and the horse suggested to me that he was a highwayman in hiding. Yet I did not wish to say so, worried that it might provoke a deadly response. All I said was, "No, sir. I know nothing about you."

"My name is Sandys. Mr. Sandys. That name mean anything to you?"

"No, sir."

"You just came from Melcombe. Know anyone, see anyone looking for me? Someone mouthing my name?"

"I heard nothing, sir."

"What about Mr. Jonathan Wild? Have you heard of him?"

I shook my head.

"'Thief-taker general of Great Britain and Ireland,' he calls himself. Don't believe it. He's the chief thief of the nation. You'd be wise to keep far away from him. If he puts your name in his book, you belong to him. He's the devil's own serpent."

Mr. Sandys grimaced and shook his head—as if to clear away ugly thoughts. Then he leaned forward and added, "He's searching for me and I don't intend to let him find me."

"I hope you succeed, sir." Though I knew nothing of who this Mr. Wild was, or why he might be pursuing Mr. Sandys, I wasn't going to ask.

Mr. Sandys rubbed his face all over, briefly shut his eyes, all of which suggested great weariness and desperation. "Perhaps," he said, "it shows your intelligence that you don't say more." He studied me silently for a few moments.

"What I will tell you," he resumed, "is the stagecoach you're intending to board will go by here a little past six o'clock in the morning. If you had gotten on it at the Bear Inn, the likelihood of your getting past this place would have been very small."

"Why, sir?"

"It would have been stopped."

"By . . . you?"

He nodded and grinned and by so doing acknowledged he was a highwayman. When he said no more, I found courage enough to say, "I think I should go, sir. I have to get to London." I added, "If I have to, I can walk."

"Not cow-hearted, are you? Not afraid of the dark." He leaned in. "You afraid of me?"

"Yes, sir. I am."

He considered this for a moment and then shrugged. "You've got good reason to be." He was silent for a moment. Then he said, "Mind, if I let you go, and you go back to town and impeach me, do you know what I'll do?"

"No sir."

He pointed his pistol at me again. "I'll use this. In some way or in some fashion, you'd be dead. Do you believe me?"

"Oh yes, sir, absolutely." Out of habit I gave him my smile.

He studied me another long while. "How old are you, anyway?"

"Twelve, sir."

"Older than I thought." Pistol in hand, he continued to stare at me across the fire. "Tell you what: I'm going to let you go."

"Oh, sir, thank you."

"But only with conditions. If you keep to this here Dorchester Road you'll reach the Swan Inn. Kept by my widowed mother. It's where I'm intending to go, but I need be sure it's absolutely safe. That no one is waiting for me there. Before I let you go you must swear to go to her."

"Yes, sir," I said instantly. "I swear."

"Stand up."

I did.

"Give me your hat."

I did that, too.

He tore off some of his ragged sleeve lace and tucked it into my hatband. Handing the hat back, he said, "Leave that lace where I put it. Go to the inn. If there's an elderly woman there, that's my mother. The lace will tell her I'm near. She made it, so she'll recognize it. If she's alone—mind! Only if she's alone!—tell her where I am. If it's safe she'll come for me. But, heed me, if anyone else is there, say nothing. Nothing! Not about the lace or me. Understand, nothing," he repeated, jiggling his pistol by way of emphasis.

I said, "Might that . . . Mr. Wild you spoke about, sir,

might he be there?" I was wondering if I was going into worse danger.

"Not a chance. Wild does nothing himself, but gets others to do his filthy work." That said, he reached into his pocket and drew out two shillings and offered them to me. "Here! This should buy you some food at the inn," he said, as if bestowing a generous gift to me. I thought it odd: he, making a gift of the money he stole from me, money I had taken from *The Rose in June*. And I was to give it to his mother.

"Get on then," he said. "To the Swan Inn."

"Yes, sir," I said, taking the money.

"Don't forget: Tell anyone about me other than my mother—any information against me—repeat what will happen to you."

"You'll kill me, sir."

"By bloody stones, I will! Now, get on before I change my mind."

I turned and fairly raced out of the old fort onto the Dorchester Road, the moonlight bright enough to illuminate my way.

Fearful that this Mr. Sandys might change his mind and come after me, I kept looking back over my shoulder, listening for the sound of a horse.

As for my promised mission to go to the Swan Inn, the savage Mr. Sandys had made me feel I must. Yes, my intent was to get as far and as fast away from him. But I was truly famished and had hopes that when I reached the inn I could at least secure some food. Except for that mouthful of old cheese, I hadn't eaten for two days.

As I continued going along the road, I hugged myself tightly within my great coat against the deepening cold, and moved as fast as I could. I don't know how long I had been going before I heard hoofbeats behind me. Terrified that Mr. Sandys had changed his mind and was coming to shoot me, I hurried off the road and flung myself upon the ground in hopes I would not be seen.

As the horse galloped by, I peeked up.

The rider's speed was too fast and the moonlight not quite strong enough for me to be sure who it was. I didn't think it Mr. Sandys. But whoever he was, he took no note of me. For my own part, as the horse flashed by, I noted a bright bridle decoration shaped like a star, which made me wish I had taken a better look at Mr. Sandys's horse.

Back on my feet, I watched the rider gallop out of sight. As I stood there, I convinced myself that, whoever he was, he had nothing to do with me. Besides, I had left Melcombe and save that, I had lost money, I had dealt with a highwayman and come away unharmed. Nothing worse, I thought, could happen.

I could not have been more wrong.

CHAPTER TWENTY-SEVEN

My Adventures at the Swan Inn.

I continued along the road, hands deep in coat pockets clutching my two shillings, occasionally wiping my cold nose. Happily, as I walked, that passing rider was the only person I saw, though now and again I saw dark houses. Even if I had seen a light—which I did not—I felt obliged to Mr. Sandys to reach the Swan. That is to say, I was sufficiently convinced of his violence to think it wise to keep our agreement. For his sake, I hoped that person he spoke of—that Mr. Wild who so clearly frightened him—would not find him. Or me. The very name, Wild, did not suggest benevolence.

Most of all, hunger was on my mind and in my belly, so I was eager to get to the inn.

I am not sure how long I walked—it might have been as long as two hours—the night ever colder—when I saw some wavering light ahead of me. Praying it was the inn, I used such strength as remained to sprint forward. Within moments I was standing before a building.

The pale yellow moonlight revealed an old wooden house with a thatched roof. There was a big, central door split in half, in the Dutch fashion. Over that door hung a broken carving of a whitish swan, the long neck missing. It took no imagination but much relief to believe I had reached the Swan Inn, tottering though it might be.

On both sides of its central door were windows, both of which had multitudes of small diamond panes, each pane glowing from what I took to be a hearth fire inside. A saddled horse was tied to a hitching post. With sudden unease I noticed the bridle, which bore that star-shaped bosset I had seen on the horse that had passed me on the road. In other words, that rider had come to this inn. I much preferred to think it was not Mr. Sandys's horse, but I couldn't be sure. What if it was the man who was hunting him, that Mr. Wild?

As I stood before the door, fingering my coins and trying to build some boldness, I smelled burning wood. That promised warmth. I also smelled cooking. Then I heard a man's voice singing loudly.

Hark! I hear the sound of coaches!
The hour of attack approaches,

To your arms, brave boys, and loud.
See the ball I hold!
Let the alchemists toil like asses,
Our fire their fire surpasses,
And turns all our lead to gold!

So hark, I hear the sound of—

To me, such singing suggested that a fair number of people were within, which I took as another good sign. Besides, by that time my stomach was all but barking with hunger.

I rapped on the door. On the instant, the singing stopped and was followed by silence. Momentarily, the top part of the door swung open. A woman stood looking out, lantern in hand.

She was an elderly woman, her tousled gray hair not contained by her white mobcap. The light of her lantern revealed distrustful eyes and a long and ruddy face full of tension. Her free hand was clutching a shawl against the cold.

I assumed that this was Mr. Sandys's mother, the one to whom I was supposed to deliver his message. I would have told her right off, but the singing I heard informed me that someone else was there, and I had expressly been ordered that the message must be given privately.

Holding up the lantern, the woman peered out to see who was at her door. I had the distinct impression that she was expecting someone.

"What do you want?" she said.

I hastily pulled off my hat, gave her my cheerful smile, and said, "Please, madam, I'm just a boy on the road to London."

"London's far away," she said, her voice heavy with suspicion.

"Yes, madam, I know it only too well."

Momentarily, she looked past me. "Are you alone?"

"Yes, madam."

"Are you begging?"

"Please, madam, I'm hungry and I can pay for food."

"Can you?"

I pulled the two shillings Mr. Sandys had given me from my pocket and held them out.

Apparently convinced I was alone and worthy of her custom, the woman stepped back and opened the bottom half of the door.

"Come in then," she said, but I noted she again looked beyond me to make sure I was truly unaccompanied. Her gaze was so intense I, too, peeped around.

No one was there.

Hat in hand, I stepped into a small, warm room whose well-worn wooden floor was smooth but uneven. Overhead were large square beams, coated with soot. At the end of the room was a hearth in which a low fire was burning. For the most part, the fire consisted of twinkling embers, whose flickering cast shadows that seemed to dance upon the walls.

Against two walls were settles with enough room for four men to sit on each. In the center of the room, two small square tables, with chairs set around. A young man was seated at one of the tables, with a cup and bowl before him, as well as a half-eaten loaf of bread. He was wearing a green jacket with buttons from neck to hem, plus fine lace at his wide cuffs. His hat was ornamented with a white feather.

He was the same man I'd seen talking to Mr. Bartholomew outside the guild hall earlier in the day.

Was this young man that Mr. Wild, whom Mr. Sandys spoke about? The one he said was hunting him? Then it struck me: perhaps at the behest of Mr. Bartholomew, this young man was looking for me. I hardly knew what to do—stay or bolt, the more so since on the table where he sat lay two fine pistols.

But when the young man turned toward me, I saw not so much as a glimmer of recognition or hostility in his eyes. Unless he was hiding his knowledge of me with great shrewdness, his gaze appeared to be little more than casual curiosity. I chose to think his presence had nothing to do with me and took him for a young gentleman, clean shaven and dressed elegantly. How utterly different was his appearance and manner in contrast to Mr. Sandys. To be sure, he was out of place in this small country inn, but I told myself he was probably just pausing for warm refreshment on a cold night.

The young man and woman gazed at me with looks of interest, as if unsure what to make of an unaccompanied and hungry boy appearing out of the night.

As I stood there, not knowing what to say, I saw the woman's eyes glance at my hat, which I had in my hand. The fragment of lace cuff, put there by Mr. Sandys, was surely visible. I couldn't be certain if the woman saw it, for she quickly shifted her eyes away. Yet the look in her eyes changed, becoming even more watchful. I decided she had noticed the lace.

"Where are you from, boy?" she asked.

"Melcombe Regis, madam."

"Not so far. And you say you are on your way to London?"

"Yes, madam."

"I've just come from there," said the young man with an unstinting smile that suggested he was at great ease with the world. "On the way I paused at the Bear Inn. The innkeeper told me he had noticed a solitary person hurrying along the road. Was that you?"

My heart thumped but I managed to say, "I don't know, sir."

"Are you," he asked, "intending to walk all the way to London?"

"Yes, sir."

"A long journey."

"Yes, sir," I returned, continuing to stand there, hat in hand, wishing for an easier welcome.

"And you travel at night," said the woman. "Why so? And your parents? What of them?"

"My father," I said, "who is in London, summoned me in haste, which is why I'm going there. My mother died long ago." Unable to hold back, I said, "Please, madam, I'm very hungry."

"A lonely boy and hungry at that," said the woman with what sounded at last like some kindness. "It'll cost you a shilling for supper, bed, and then breakfast before you go on in the morning."

Though she was speaking to me, she kept glancing at the young man. It was as if she had to ask his permission to make the offer.

"Go on," said the young man, "feed him. He looks fairly famished."

The woman's proposal seemed expensive fare to me, but I had neither desire nor strength to bargain. I held out a coin. She took it and put it in her apron pocket.

"Sit here," she said, and gestured to the empty table.

When I did—putting my hat on the floor—she left the room, but not without another darting, anxious look at the young man. It was as if they were engaged in some private give-and-take, though I had no idea what it might be.

The young man picked up his half-eaten loaf from his table and placed it before me. "You can begin with this," he said, his smile suggesting he found me amusing.

"Thank you, sir," I said. Appreciating his kindness and his easy smile, I took up the bread and began to devour it.

The young man laughed. "When did you eat last, boy?"

"This afternoon, sir. A piece of cheese."

"And before that?"

"A goodly while, sir," I said.

"Why," he asked, "were you at Melcombe?"

"I live there," I said and bit off another large piece of bread.

"Were you there when the storm struck?" he asked.

I nodded.

"Did you hear about the wreck?"

It was suddenly hard to swallow the bread. Perhaps Mr. Bartholomew had told him about me.

"The customs master told me the ship was looted," said the young man, his eyes steady on me. "Did you have a hand in that? Is that why you're on the road at night?"

CHAPTER TWENTY-EIGHT

Which Concerns Certain Talk at the Swan Inn.

Though the young man smiled when he asked his question I was so startled I had to struggle to resume my smile. Yet I saw no accusation in his face, merely casual interest. I preferred to believe he was that kind of adult who finds young people a general source of amusement.

The woman came back with a great bowl of steaming stew. She set it down before me along with a wooden spoon and more bread. As I ate with gusto, she stepped back to watch me, now and again glancing nervously at the young man while also shifting her eyes toward the door.

I continued to consume the food while the two adults watched me as if the rate of my eating was a marvel to behold. But I was equally sure they wished to ask me something.

Sure enough, the young man said, "Tell me—between mouthfuls—did you see anyone on the road?"

I glanced up from my bowl. The woman's eyes were fixed on me.

"No, sir," I said, remembering Mr. Sandys's warning. "No one."

"Not even a man . . ." and the young man went on to describe Mr. Sandys quite neatly.

As he spoke the woman's face paled and her fingers entwined, as if tying and untying a nub. Meanwhile, I tried to keep my face blank.

"Anyone?" persisted the young man.

"Please, sir, it was too dark to see much of anything."

Though he studied me intently, the young man kept his smile. "I like to think I can read faces," he said. "And you have as honest a young face as I've ever seen. Pure innocence. You could do wonders with a face like that."

"Thank you, sir," I said, not sure what to make of his remark.

I finished the bowl, at which point the woman filled it again. I was getting my money's worth.

At length the woman said to me, "It's late. I suggest you get to sleep."

I needed no urging. Between final gulps of food, I said, "Yes, please."

The young man laughed. "The more rest today, the quicker your step to London," he said.

"I'll fix your bed," the woman said, and once again she left the room.

I kept eating. Now and again the young man glanced at me as if making an appraisal. I tried to ignore him.

The woman returned. That was when the young man said to her, "Have you any notion as to when Mr. Sandys shall come?"

My spoon halted halfway between the bowl and my mouth.

The woman said, "What makes you think he will come?"

"I've been informed he's in the neighborhood."

"By whom?"

"There's talk in Melcombe. I assure you, madam, when a well-known highwayman passes through town, he will be noticed."

I looked into my food and began to eat faster.

"Are you so sure he's a highwayman?" said the woman.

I looked up.

"I am," said the young man with a smile demonstrating the art of saying hard things in a soft way.

The woman drew herself up stiffly. "Why should you care?"

"My sole desire, madam, is to deliver a message to Mr.

148

Sandys from Mr. Jonathan Wild. I have no doubt he would be anxious to hear it."

When that name was spoke—the person mentioned by Mr. Sandys—I could have sworn the woman winced. "And why would this Mr. Sandys need to be anxious of Mr. Wild?"

The young man laughed. "Men often are when they are on the road to Tyburn."

That time the woman's ruddy face turned pale.

I wondered where in the world that Tyburn was, but thought it safer not to ask.

By way of ending that conversation, the young man shifted about so that he faced the door, as if wanting to be the first to see who might come in. He also moved his pistols closer to his hands. He even cocked them.

The woman quickly turned to me and said, "Come along, boy. Your bed is ready."

I hastily finished off the stew. Then I allowed myself to be led into a small, windowless room—a closet really—at the back of the house, with a high, narrow bed, heaped with blankets.

As she closed the door behind us, I put my hat on the bed. The moment I did, she reached out and plucked the bit of lace from the hatband.

"Where did you get this?" she asked, her voice low, strained.

Whispering, I said, "Mr. Sandys gave it to me. He told me you should have it."

"Where is he?"

"At Mountjoy Fort. He asked me to tell you he's there. That you might come and fetch him."

Clutching the lace bit in her fist, the woman went to the doorway only to pause. "Say nothing to that man." She pointed toward the front room.

"Please, then madam, tell me: Who is this Mr. Wild?"

"No one you'll want to know," she said.

"And Tyburn? Where is that?"

"It's the London gallows," she said. "The triple tree." Taking her lamp and the lace, she left me in the dark, in more ways than one.

I threw off my coat and boots, climbed into the bed, and burrowed under the blankets like a mole in his tunnel. Then I gave myself over to think out the long day.

How very far did the poorhouse seem to be. I thought more of what Mr. Sandys, his mother, and the young man might have in common. The best I could come up with was that they were engaged in something unlawful. I knew Mr. Sandys was a highwayman. And here the young man was waiting for Mr. Sandys, with cocked pistols and a warning. How could he—I wondered—know enough about him so as to come to this inn? What business did he have with Mr. Bartholomew in Melcombe? Was he coming to arrest Mr. Sandys? And why did this Mr. Wild hover over all?

My situation called to mind those times I played in the sea along Melcombe's beaches: The surface of the water might appear to be completely calm, but a dangerous undertow could pull you down at any moment and drag you into deep danger.

I therefore made up my mind to leave the Swan Inn as early and as fast in the morning as I could and hurry on to London. So resolved it was not long before fatigue overtook me and I fell asleep quite quickly.

It was the sound of gunshots that woke me.

CHAPTER TWENTY-NINE

In Which I Try to Escape.

The gunshots came in such rapid succession, and from such a great distance, I was not sure I heard them, being asleep. I lay abed, waiting to hear more. When no further sounds came, I decided it had been a dream, thoughts stirred by Mr. Sandys as well as the young man aiming pistols at me the night previous.

Since my small room had no windows, I could not judge the sun and therefore the time. I only knew I felt I had slept enough, and despite my unusual awakening, I felt restored. I decided that whatever the hour, I would put my resolution about leaving into action and depart as quickly as possible.

I groped for my coat and hat and put them on but left off my boots, so I could walk quietly. Then I stepped down the hall toward the inn's main room. Even before

I emerged from the hall, I saw pinkish light streaming through those diamond-paned front windows, which allowed me to perceive the time to be shortly after dawn. I recalled ruefully that was about the time the stagecoach left Melcombe, the one I had wished to be on.

As soon as I stepped into the main room, I saw the young man. He appeared to be asleep with his bowed head upon his crossed arms at the table where he had been the night before. I walked softly and had barely gone halfway across the room when he sat up. Before I could react, his two pistols were in hand and both were aimed at me.

Shocked, I could do nothing but stand there, mouth agape.

The next instant, the young man grinned as if it all had been a jest. He put his pistols on the table.

"Not only do I have uncommon sharp ears and quick triggers," he said, "my reputation for aiming wonderfully true is renowned. It's not a good idea to sneak about me like that, lad."

"I wasn't intending to sneak, sir," I said, which was not quite true.

"Did those gunshots wake you?" he asked.

"No, sir," I lied again. "Were you shooting?"

"No, not I," he said, "but I suspect we shall learn more before long." He glanced down. "You have no shoes. Were you going to walk that way to London?"

"I didn't wish to disturb anyone, sir."

Momentarily serious, he considered me for a moment. "Do you know where your father is residing in London?"

I shook my head.

"Then how do you expect to find him?"

"I'm not sure."

"What kind of money do you have?"

I dug into my pocket and held out my sole remaining shilling.

"Without money," he said, "London is hell. With money it is paradise." He laughed. "Consider that a sermon. I suggest you have some breakfast before you go. You've paid a great deal for it and you're not likely to eat again for a while."

I had to admit that was a good idea. What's more, I rather appreciated the young man's good cheer. I found him quite friendly and agreeable, a great contrast to the men with whom I had been dealing of late.

When I pulled on my boots and took a place at the empty table, the young man stood up and poked at the hearth fire with an iron rod there for that purpose. The flames flared. The room warmed. Then he came back to the table and inspected his pistols. Though I guessed he was still waiting for Mr. Sandys, I said nothing.

After a while the woman who kept the inn came into

the room. Seeing the young man, she stopped. "Still here," she said.

"I am."

"I pray he will not come."

"I've never known two men to pray for the same things."

"Did you hear gunshots?" she asked.

"I did." The young man looked at me and grinned.

They said no more to each other but I sensed the strain between them.

The woman turned to me. "Will you want some breakfast, boy?"

"Yes, madam, please."

She went out of the room.

The young man looked to me and said, "If you get to London, how will you feed yourself?"

"My father."

"You just told me you didn't know how to find him."

"I have to try, sir," I said.

"There are many ways a boy can earn his keep."

"I hope so, sir."

"Last night I mentioned Mr. Jonathan Wild. Do you know who he is?"

"No, sir," I said, not wishing to share what had been told to me by Mr. Sandys.

"Wild is one of the great men in England. He always has jobs for boys. Search him out when you reach London. You may find him at the sign of the King's Head Inn. On Ship Court near the prison. The ward is known as Old Bailey, near the law courts, St. Paul's Cathedral, and New-gate Prison. You have one shilling left. Give it to me."

I did as I was told.

He pulled a dagger from his boot and scratched an *X* on the face of the coin, then handed it back to me. "When you see Mr. Wild, give him that and tell him Captain Billy Hawkes—that's me—sent you. He'll treat you well."

I was impressed by his kindness.

The next moment, there was a great rattling noise coming from outside, the sound of galloping horses, creaking leather, the jangle of chains.

Captain Hawkes said, "The stagecoach from Mel-combe to London."

I must have looked regretful, for he said, "Do you wish you were on it?"

"Yes, sir."

He gave his easy smile. "But you have so little money."

I shrugged.

"If you had been on the stage you might have lost even that."

"What do you mean?"

"Those gunshots. I suspect someone was attempting to rob the coach."

I must have looked disconcerted because he laughed. "I believe you heard me say I am waiting for Mr. Sandys. Do you know why?"

"No, sir."

"Mr. Wild knows every thief in England. Knows where they are and what they do. I have the honor to be one of Mr. Wild's captains. Mr. Sandys considers himself to be a gentleman of the road and was once in the employ of Mr. Wild."

At that moment the woman came back, bringing two large slices of bread and a bowl of hot milk. She placed them on the table where I was sitting. I began to eat fast, more eager than ever to leave.

Captain Hawkes resumed his restless waiting, now and again fingering his pistols.

Quite suddenly, the door burst open.

CHAPTER THIRTY

In Which I Reveal Who Was at the Door.

Standing on the threshold was Mr. Sandys. He leaned hard against the door frame, his left hand clutching his right shoulder, his face pale and haggard.

On the instant, Captain Hawkes snatched up his pistols and aimed them at the man. Mr. Sandys looked at him with what seemed resigned disgust. Then he turned to me with an accusatory look.

The woman, seeing her son, gave a cry and rushed forward, put her arms about him, and helped him into a chair. He sat heavily, letting forth something of a groan. She then struggled to remove his jacket, which was not easy, for it caused him much pain. When she finally drew the jacket off, the sleeve of Mr. Sandys's shirt was stained red.

In all this no words were spoken, but it was clear that

Mr. Sandys had been wounded. Naturally, I thought of the shots I'd heard.

Captain Hawkes continued to stand there, pistols in hand, watching Mr. Sandys.

The woman hurried out of the room.

Only then did Hawkes speak. "The coach driver was armed, then?" he said to Mr. Sandys.

The highwayman nodded. It was a worn-out motion and suggested that he was suffering.

"Sandys, you're a fool to work alone," said the captain. "It takes more skill than you have."

Mr. Sandys stared angrily at me and for a moment I thought he was about to reveal that he and I had met. Perhaps he thought better of it for he turned back to Hawkes and said, "Why are you here?"

Captain Hawkes said, "Mr. Wild was informed you were in the area. He sent me here and asked me to deliver a message."

"Speak it then," said Mr. Sandys. He was staring at the ground, as if resigned.

The woman came back with a bowl of water and a cloth. She pulled away Mr. Sandys's bloody sleeve and began to wash the wound.

Captain Hawkes said, "You do not have Mr. Wild's permission to be on the roads. Moreover, he requires you to report to him."

"In London. At the King's Head?"

Hawkes nodded.

"What will Wild do for me?"

"You can guess as well as me."

"He'll take out his book," said Sandys, "and put a double cross next to my name."

"You'll have to take your chances."

Mr. Sandys pointed to me. "Is this boy one of Wild's coves?"

"Not yet, but I hope he will be."

With that, Captain Hawkes turned to the woman. "I thank you for your hospitality, madam." He bowed and flourished his feathered hat. To me, he smiled and made another bow. "Boy, I hope we shall meet again. Once more, I urge you to visit Mr. Wild."

With that Captain Hawkes left the inn.

What was clear to me now was this: Mr. Sandys had attempted to rob the stagecoach, the same coach I had planned to be on. He had been held off, wounded by an armed guard—the gunshots I heard—and was escaping to where his mother lived, the Swan Inn.

Furthermore, Captain Hawkes was connected to the highwayman, and had come to give him a warning from this Mr. Jonathan Wild, the man Sandys told me was "the chief thief of the nation."

In short, I had stumbled upon a nest of thieves and

their disputes. Was I to be one of them? Or perhaps I already was one after taking those shillings. I believed my father had gone for Charity's sake, but how I wished—with a dab of anger—he had not left me as he had done.

Mr. Sandys turned to me savagely with his wild eyes. "Did you tell him about me?" he fairly hissed.

The woman, who was dressing the wound, said, "He spoke only to me."

Sandys relaxed. "Good enough," he muttered.

"Will you go to Wild?" she asked her son.

"He'll have me hanged. I need to get away. To the colonies in America. I'll be safe there."

Wishing to learn no more, I stood up. "Please. I have to go."

"Still to London?" said Mr. Sandys.

"Yes, sir."

He put his good hand into his pocket and to my surprise he drew out a fistful of shillings. "Here. Take your money back. You've played fair. You can't walk to London. It's too far. Continue along the Dorchester Road and catch tomorrow's coach. But if you reach the city, be warned: I'm giving you those shillings for only one reason. So you don't have to go to Wild. He'll call you his friend and then hang you for the reward."

"Thank you, sir," I said, taking the money and quickly moving toward the door. Before I reached it his mother handed me a penny's worth of bread. "To eat upon the road," she said. Thus with Mr. Sandys's warning in my ears, and the bread stuffed in my pocket, I left the Swan Inn.

Once outside, I saw that Captain Hawkes's horse was no longer at the hitching rail. Relieved to find him gone, I was pleased to take to the road. My sole resolution—other than to get to London—was to have nothing to do with such thieves. That, I told myself, should be easy enough.

Alas, when you talk to yourself, there's no one to say that you are wrong.

CHAPTER THIRTY-ONE

In Which, Even as I Made My Way to London, Something Startling Happens.

I walked fast, wondering how long I would need to travel before I could pause and wait for the next London coach. As I went along I constantly reached into my pocket to make sure my shillings remained. I did pass inns now and again. At each, I inquired if the London stage stopped there, only to be told I must continue north to an inn called the Anchor.

I continued thus for the better part of the day. At one point, sitting by the side of the road, I ate some of the bread Mr. Sandys's mother gave me while reviewing my father's now crumpled letter.

I still could not configure what the word "mXXXXXd" meant. Charity: not likely mothered, marbled, or matured. What had called my father to London with such urgency?

All in all, I believe I walked some fifteen miles until I reached the Anchor Inn. It announced itself by its swinging sign, which consisted of the image of an anchor, entwined by the word "Hope."

It was bigger than the Swan, but other than having a large stable, it did not seem unusual in any way. Wanting to reserve all the money I had, I asked for no food but only for some water. The innkeepers, a man and his wife, were perfectly agreeable. When I inquired and was told a London stage would arrive next morning, I offered to buy my London ticket then and there.

"Twenty shillings inside the coach," I was informed, and rather smugly, too, as if doubting I could pay it. "Fifteen on the top, and ten to be in the basket."

Naturally, I opted for the cheapest option, the basket—commonly known as a "rumble tumble"—and paid for my ticket.

Seeing me a legitimate customer, the innkeepers, with newfound kindness—for it is an old truth that money opens hearts as well as doors—gave me a penny's worth of fusty bread and told me I was free to wait about until the next day. For the most part I stayed in the inn's main room, where local folk came and went.

Idling in a corner, I heard much talk about a gang of highwaymen recently infesting the area, masked men who, though courteous, took everything passengers had. It was what Mr. Webber's boy at the Bear Inn had warned me about. I assumed, too, they were talking about Mr. Sandys. But you may be sure I only listened, and revealed nothing.

That night I slept in the inn's stables, knowing that when the morning coach stopped I'd be able to claim my place. Sure enough it arrived mid-morning. As soon as it came, the stable-nag, the boy employed by the inn, worked to change the horses.

The stagecoach was little more than an enclosed square box—maybe twelve feet high—on four large wheels. This one was driven by an arrangement of horses known as a unicorn, which is to say, three horses, with a postilion (a rider) on the lead horse. On the top, the foremost seat of the carriage was occupied by the coachman, who carried a whip and, I was glad to note, a blunderbuss.

With its short barrel, a blunderbuss can fire a fistful of shot at a short range. It is not known for precise shooting, but is the kind of gun whose scattershot is enough to drive off the likes of Mr. Sandys. No doubt it was that which had wounded him.

The carriage, when it reached the Anchor, carried two passengers inside, a wealthy man and his wife. There were two other men on the top, merchants, clinging to the rails provided for them. At the rear of the carriage proper— a common arrangement—was a large wicker basket attached to the coach, hanging between the wheels. That basket, the rumble tumble, was known for being the cheapest ride, and the most uncomfortable.

When I gave the coachman my ticket, he told me I might take my place. Only then did I discover that an immense fat man was already wedged deep within the basket, asleep and reeking of gin. I could no more shift him than I might have moved the carcass of a dead whale. The best I could do was wedge myself in a tight corner, for this bloated man was unwilling to share, and perhaps incapable of doing so, even the smallest space.

The horses having been changed, the passengers in place, on top, within the coach, and in the basket behind, there was a "Hallo" from the coachman, and off we went.

It is said that a person can walk three miles an hour and sustain such a pace while avoiding the ruts and holes in the roads. By way of contrast, such a coach as I was in could go four miles an hour, but that was when the road was smooth. English roads were almost never smooth. At best their dirt surfaces were broken, rutted, and gouged, level stretches being scarce as unicorns.

Thus the coach bounced and butted, shook and swayed, rattled and creaked, almost every inch of the way. There were moments when the coach, rolling into holes, seemed to drop off a cliff, landing at the bottom with a severe thump, enough to rearrange one's every bone. At such times my bulging basket companion would fall against me and compress me, or so it felt, into a much smaller size than I already was. My good-natured smiles were useless. It took shoves, pinches, and such slight strength as I possessed to reclaim my small space.

Then there were those times when going uphill that all the men must disembark (never my drunken basket mate) to lighten the load, or to help push the coach along. The task was worse when we were stuck in mud. As for the cold . . .

The basket in which I sat exaggerated all these conditions. I nonetheless remained there with my hat pulled low, my oversized coat tight, hugging my knees, compressed into a corner by my massive basket mate. We traveled in this fashion, until I began to wish I had walked. Is there any inconvenience such as convenience gone badly?

It was late afternoon, and we were going through a patch of forest, when the coach suddenly stopped. All became still. Curious to know the reason, I hauled myself into a standing position so I could look forward over the top of the coach.

Some twenty yards ahead in the middle of the road, blocking the way, was a man astride a horse. He had a black cloak about his shoulders—hiding his garments—and a black mask over his eyes. He wore no hat. The mask in itself was a capital offence, which is to say, the law stated that by wearing one he could be hanged. What's more, in his hands he brandished a pair of pistols and he was aiming them at the coach.

"Stand and deliver!" he commanded.

Even as I looked on, there was a flash of flame issuing from one of the highwayman's pistols followed almost instantly by a loud *bang!* and a puff of smoke. The next moment there came a sharp cry, after which I saw a blunderbuss drop to the ground.

Whoever the man was, he was a superb shot.

"Tell all your passengers to come upon the road," called the masked man as he cantered forward on his horse.

The coachman shouted, "Get out! All of you! If you value your life!"

Intimidated and terrified, and not considering resisting for a moment, I leaped out of the basket onto the road and held my hands high.

CHAPTER THIRTY-TWO

I Provide an Account of a Robbery.

The two men who had been on top of the coach dropped down in almost equal haste. They were followed by the wealthy man and his wife from inside the carriage. Finally, with much grunting and moaning, the large man who shared my basket actually bestirred himself and climbed out. The coachman—who was holding a bloody hand—got down as well, as did the postilion. All were very frightened.

"Line up side by side by the edge of the road," was the next command from the highwayman. "Place all your money, jewelry, and watches at your feet."

Very soon there was a small mound of money and watches heaped before each passenger. In front of the wealthy couple was a bag of I knew not what—perhaps jewelry—plus a large snuffbox. It looked to be gold.

The rider wheeled his horse around and deftly dismounted, his cape billowing so he looked like a raven fluttering down to earth. In one hand he held a pistol. In his other hand he had an open sack.

"Please be so kind as to put your goods into this bag," he said, and proceeded along the row of unhappy passengers. I, with equal reluctance, took out my shillings and laid them at my feet.

We stood there, all in a row, myself included, eyes cast down, fearful of looking at the thief since it was common knowledge that highwaymen often killed witnesses who might identify them.

"And what is your name and position?" the highwayman asked the first man in line.

"John . . . Kolbert, gentleman," said the man with haughty reluctance even as he put his possessions into the highwayman's bag.

"Thank you, sir," said the highwayman and passed on down the line, inquiring politely of each of the people he was robbing.

I was at the end of the line. As he held out his now almost full bag for my contribution, I dropped in my coins. I dared not look up at his masked face, but instead stared at his chest. In so doing I noticed his green jacket with buttons from neck to hem, as well as his fine cuff lace, all of which I recognized. The highwayman was none other than Captain Billy Hawkes.

Such was my surprise I looked up. The highwayman—Captain Hawkes—grinned. He did not bother to ask me who I was.

The next moment, he called out, "Except for this boy, you may all get back in the coach and proceed."

You might think someone—passengers, coachman, or postilion—would protest this kidnapping of me, a boy, but they were only too happy to escape with their lives. Of course the notion "women and children first" is a rarity. Men first and children last, is what I have mostly observed.

In any case, the passengers—minus me—being all on board, the coachman gave a loud call, the postilion spurred his horse, and the carriage rattled off.

So it was that I was left entirely alone with Captain Hawkes, with me wondering if he was going to treat me as a dangerous witness to his deed.

CHAPTER THIRTY-THREE

A Short Chapter, Which Nonetheless Contains Some Important Ideas.

If you have followed my story—and I hope you have not skipped a single word because I have labored extremely hard on each and every one—you should have noted that every time I move forward, I am thwarted by an adult. I hasten to say I was not one of those young people who claimed that if I were only left alone by grown-ups, all would be well. No. I simply would have asked the older people who entered my life—those who, in fact, took charge of my life—that they might have consulted me as to what I might have preferred.

The outcomes might have been different.

On the other hand, I would not like you to think me passive. I beg you to recall that I was being continually threatened or had pistols leveled at me by older people.

What would you have me do? Turn upon my tormentors and attack them? Consider: How long would I have survived?

No, I understood my position very well: It would take wits to free myself from these tormentors.

Nonetheless, there I was: the London stagecoach gone and me standing on the side of the road, alone with the highwayman, Captain Billy Hawkes.

I could no longer smile. Rather, I was equal parts disgust and despair.

"I was hoping you'd be on that coach," said Captain Hawkes as he removed the mask from his face so there was absolutely no doubt as to who he was.

The best return I could summon up was a glum, "Please, sir, why?"

The captain offered up his most engaging smile. "When I saw you at that inn, alone and without funds, you struck me as brave. I took a liking to you. How did you get on the coach?"

"Mr. Sandys gave me money."

"That speaks better of him than I thought. But I promise you, I can do much better."

"Please, sir, I'd rather do better by myself."

He laughed. "You have no choice. Since you know who I am, I can't hazard having you provide information against me. You'll have to do as I tell you. But rest assured: I wish you no harm. Do as I say and things will go well. To begin, I need you to get up on my horse and ride with me."

So it was that I became Captain Hawkes's prisoner.

When we consider knaves and villains we want them to have cruel faces, uncivil tongues, as if good manners were true mirrors of good souls. I say, better to judge men and women by what they do than how they appear, for a smooth face may be but a mask for sin. There is nothing uglier than a rogue with an engaging smile. And, make no mistake, Captain Hawkes was a rogue. Yet he always spoke with soothing cheerfulness and a laughter-loving smile, the perfect portrait of a polite gentleman.

You must understand that from this time forward, I was never to be out of his control. Still, from the same moment the captain took charge of me I was resolved to regain my liberty. Everything I did was done out of my desire and design to regain my freedom.

Now I shall tell you how well I succeeded.

CHAPTER THIRTY-FOUR

In Which I Recount My Time with Captain Hawkes.

The captain got on his horse, his bag of stolen money and goods attached to his saddle. Then he reached down, grasped my hand and hauled me up, so that I sat before him. Quite deftly, he slipped the horse's reins over me, thus making me truly captive, and we rode off. Such was our speed, and his control of me, I could not entertain thoughts of leaping free.

"Were you still intending to go to London?" he asked as we rode along.

"Yes, sir."

"To find your father?"

"Yes, sir," I said, extremely glad I had never mentioned Charity.

"And going to Mr. Wild as I suggested?"

Not wishing to say "no," I hesitated before saying, "I have not truly considered it."

"Well," he said, "we must see him."

"I don't wish to," I said.

"You will regardless."

The horse galloped on.

I am not sure how far we went, but at some point—we were still in the forest—he turned off and followed a well-worn path among the trees and shrubs. We soon came into a clearing where three men were sitting around a small fire. Behind them were as many saddled horses, their reins fastened to trees.

As the captain and I entered the clearing, these men stood as if to show respect though I assumed that they, like Hawkes, were footpads or highwaymen. They were not dressed as finely as the captain. Instead, there was something rough and ragged about them, in posture as well as in clothing. Dirty, too. But all had pistols tucked into their belts. I understood by the deference they showed Hawkes that they were his gang and he their captain.

The first thing the captain did when we reached the clearing was fling down the bag that contained the money and goods he had taken from the stagecoach passengers. His men promptly took all of it up, and gleefully dumped the contents on the ground.

"You may divide it five ways," Hawkes announced,

grandly looking down at them from his horse. "One share for each of us, and one for Mr. Wild."

He turned to me. "How much did you put in?" he asked.

"Ten shillings, sir."

"And ten shillings for the boy," he said.

"Who's the chitty-faced cub?" called one of the men.

"What does he look like?" said the captain.

"A gentleman's charity-boy," said another.

"Exactly. Gentlemen, have you ever seen such a look of innocence? I warrant it: He shall make our fortunes."

Without further explanation, he set me down on the ground, and then dismounted. The next moment he retrieved—I know not from where—a leather thong, tied it round my wrist, and fastened it to a small tree on the edge of the clearing.

He, along with the other men, went through the money and watches he had stolen on the road. I was given my shillings back. It included the one that the captain had marked with an *X*.

"The gold snuffbox goes to Mr. Wild," Captain Hawkes announced, holding the item up to general admiration. No one objected.

The plunder shared, they all sat around the fire and Captain Hawkes talked about what he had done when he held up the coach: his manner, and the reaction of the passengers. His account brought laughter. He was one of those artful men, as I have suggested, who, even when talking of something offensive, can make you laugh. I will admit, even I laughed.

At one point a man asked, "Did you catch up with Sandys?"

"I did."

"Give him Wild's warning?"

"He has it."

"What will he do?"

"He'll have to come in."

The man shook his head ruefully. "He should never have left us."

Of course, I made no mention of Sandys's hope to flee to America. But I did note one further thing: Captain Hawkes gave no account of why he had been in Melcombe Regis, or his meeting with Mr. Bartholomew.

That remained a puzzle to me.

A little later another of the men asked Captain Hawkes, "What do you intend to do with the boy?"

"There will be another stagecoach passing through to-morrow," said the captain. "I have it on good intelligence that it will carry a good deal of money. The boy can be of use to us."

You may be sure that caught my attention.

"Why do you need him?" asked another.

"I want him to be part of us," said the captain and he turned to me. When he saw how I looked at him, wide-eyed, no doubt uncomfortable, he offered up his charming smile. Then he added to the others, "The more he is one of us, the less likely he will seek his independence."

I could have no doubts, he was going to make me, whether I wished to be or not, one of his gang.

After the men had eaten, Captain Hawkes came over to me and squatted down on his heels. "You must forgive the rudeness of these men," he said to me, as if he and I were particular high-class friends. "My work requires such associations. I promise you, my intent is to help you become a gentleman—like me."

His three men paid little attention to me, but continually shared stories that almost always had to do with how full of courage they were, and how stupid their victims were. To hear them recount their exploits—and I had no choice—they were all wealthy men, though I rather doubted they were. Else, why were they hiding in a forest, ill-clothed, waiting for their next theft? The exception was Captain Hawkes.

At one point, led by the captain, they sang:

Hark! I hear the sound of coaches!
The hour of attack approaches,
To your arms, brave boys, and load.

See the ball I hold!
Let the alchemists toil like asses,
Our fire their fire surpasses,
And turns all our lead to gold!

It was only when the name of Mr. Wild was mentioned that they grew less jolly. When Captain Hawkes spoke of him, the others listened with care, their faces tinged with concern. My perception of Mr. Wild continued to grow large until I began to imagine him as a ferocious giant, who towered and controlled such men as these. "Tomorrow, after we deal with this coach," Captain Hawkes announced, "Then I must make a delivery to Mr. Wild in London. When I go, you will need to stay hidden."

"What about the boy?" someone asked.

"He'll come with me." The captain glanced at me, still tethered to a tree, and gave his generous smile.

That meant that I was going to London. Not believing I had cause to be pleased, I did not return the smile. Rather, I wondered what reason the captain had for wanting me to go.

I was fed uncommonly well on what I gather was poached venison. Poaching was another serious breaking of the law. From all I had seen of Captain Hawkes, he could, if brought to trial, have been condemned to being hanged many times over.

That night I slept on the ground, part of the thieves' encampment. I had never done so before and I found the hard ground unpleasant. Not only did I twist and turn in search of comfort, I kept trying to untie the leather cord that bound me. But my fingers were incapable of pulling the strands apart. So there was nothing for me to do but wait for the next day to discover how Captain Hawkes intended to make me, as he had said, "part of us."

CHAPTER THIRTY-FIVE

In Which I Learn My Fate.

I'm not sure what time I woke, save that it was to the sound of men moving about and talking, and that it was so cold my breath clouded before my face. It took some moments for me to realize that I remained tied to a tree. When the captain noticed I was awake, he ordered my release though you may be sure I was held close.

I again spied about for some ways to get free, but the thieves were always near. Captain Hawkes, in particular, kept his eye on me.

The fire was stirred up. They and I sat about, getting warm and eating. The restlessness the men exhibited—constantly stretching arms, legs, and necks, along with abrupt laughter—showed more uneasiness than the night before, like soldiers right before a skirmish. It made me that much more apprehensive.

The captain laid out his plans. "I expect the stage-coach to pass through sometime about noon," he said. "We'll stop it at that narrow point. You know, where the road bends. The trees are close in. We'll be among them, two to each side. Stay masked. They are carrying a fair amount of money."

How, I wondered, did he know that?

"It will be the boy who'll stop the coach," Hawkes went on to say. He glanced at me and smiled. Into my head came the proverb on the walls of the poorhouse schoolroom-chapel:

A violent man enticeth his neighbor,
and leadeth him into the way that is not good.

"How's he going to do that?" asked one of the men.

"He'll take up a position in the middle of the road," the captain explained. "They won't be suspicious of a boy and most likely won't run him down.

"And," he added, "I believe the coachman will be armed."

Armed! I thought. Was I never to be out of danger?

After breakfasting the men lounged about, though I did see them clean and load their pistols, and check their horses.

Fearful of what might happen to me, I paced nervously, trying to decide if I should try and bolt. But the captain, pistol in hand, though he conferred with his men as if to give them courage, never took his eyes from me.

From time to time, Hawkes checked his pocket watch, and occasionally, looked up toward the sky. At one point, bread, drink, and dried meat were passed about. The captain squatting down by my side gave me a portion. I found it hard to eat. Rather, I took the opportunity to protest.

"Please, sir," I said. "I don't wish to stop the coach."

"But when the stagecoach appears, you will hail it. You've nothing to do other than stand in the road."

"But . . . what are you going to do?" I asked.

He smiled. "I think you know."

"But please, sir, I have no desire to do this."

"I'm not giving you a choice," he replied. "You want to go to London, do you not?"

"Yes, sir."

"After this business is done, I shall take you there."

"Thank you, sir, but I really don't want anything to do with the coach."

"Then consider this: There are five of us. We shall be concealed, two to each side of the road. You will be on the road—which is to say in the middle. I am determined to stop the coach one way or another. As I think you know, I am pretty sharp with my pistol."

"Yes, sir, I do know."

"Very well then: You can stop the coach, or I can stop

you. Do I make myself understood?" Most often the captain had the charm of fluttering ribbons. In that instant he changed into a sharp bayonet.

"Yes, sir," I mumbled. "I understand."

His easy smile returned. "Just know that I wish to be your teacher-friend. I intend to have grand times together."

"Yes, sir," I said, though my heart was heavy.

Perhaps an hour later the horses were brought up and saddles were adjusted. All four of the men mounted. Captain Hawkes put on his mask. The other men tied handkerchiefs over their faces. I alone was uncovered. At least, I thought, I would not be hanged for that.

"Oliver! Come up," called Hawkes. Holding out a hand he pulled me onto his horse once more.

We went through the forest in a line. The autumnal leaves were sweetly scented, the moldy earth pungent. The men were silent as the horses plodded steadily forward, noses blowing vapor, tails occasionally twitching. A lovely moment, if you ignore the fact that I was quite convinced I was going to my death.

We reached the road, and it was as the captain had described. Trees shading the road. A little beyond the spot where we stopped the road curved, so I could not know where it went. In the other direction I could see for a considerable distance. I would have no trouble noticing the stagecoach when it came.

I he men concealed themselves behind some trees on either side of the road, two to the left and one on the right. Captain Hawkes led his horse—both of us still mounted—some ways into the woods and tethered it there. The two of us—his hand tight upon my shoulder—walked back to the road.

"You must stand right here," he said, scratching a clear line in the dust with his boot toe. "You'll have an excellent view of the coach when it comes. And they of you. When you see them, stand fast and wave your hands. Shout. It will stop."

"Please, sir," I said again. "What if it . . . doesn't stop? What if the coachman is armed and shoots me? And . . . please, sir, I don't want to be a thief."

He considered me with amusement. "I thought you already were one."

Taken aback, I looked up. "What do you mean, sir?"

"Information has come to me that you already are a thief. What about those twenty-three shillings you stole from *The Rose in June?*"

My mouth hung open.

"As far as the law is concerned," he went on with a smile, "once a thief, always a thief. Your lawyer father must have taught you that. If I were to impeach you, you'd surely hang and I would receive forty pounds' reward for ensuring your conviction. I could live for a year on that. But"—he smiled—"I will protect you."

Though shocked that he knew these things, I was sure I understood: Mr. Bartholomew had told him about me and my father.

It was as if I had been required to become a thief for the second time. All very well to give cautions, but had not Father's behavior fairly forced me into terrible company?

"Now," he said, all smiles and courtesy, "just do as you're told. Be aware I shall not be far and I'll have my pistol aimed right at you." He took one of his pistols from his belt and cocked it, so that I could have no doubt about his threat. He was, I knew, a superb marksman.

With that Captain Hawkes retreated from the road and set himself behind a large bush. I doubted if the coach driver would see him, but I knew he was there.

There I stood, quite alone though very much aware that I was not alone. While I kept my eyes upon the road, I kept thinking of what the captain had said; that he knew I was a thief. That he could—if he chose—turn me in for a large reward. It utterly bejuggled my mind that he knew so much about me.

I was still struggling to grasp why Mr. Bartholomew would tell him about me, when I saw the stagecoach appear far down the road.

CHAPTER THIRTY-SIX

In Which I Have an Unexpected Meeting.

The instant I saw the coach, my overwhelming desire was to flee. Hasty glances to the side of the road were all I needed to remind myself that the captain was lurking there, and what he promised to do if I budged so much as an inch from the line he had toed. My choice was clear: I could be shot for refusing to help rob the coach, or be hanged for my foolish fault in taking those shillings when desperate. Or I could be run over by the coach. Oh, the folly of misjudgment!

The other option was to help stop the coach and look for another chance to escape from Captain Hawkes. Since what I most wanted to do was continue living, that was my choice.

I therefore did not budge but kept my eyes on the advancing coach. At first it appeared small, enveloped in a whirly-wind of brown dust. Then, as it rushed forward, I made out the lead horse, the postilion upon him, then the two other horses and the coach right behind.

As I stood there, the stagecoach continued to rush on but then no danger moves so fast as that which endangers you. It was coming right at me, me so small and it so large, the horses immense so that I was utterly petrified. The closer the stagecoach drew, the more impaled I was to where I stood.

With considerable effort, I finally raised both my hands and began to wave. The coach continued to race on so that my ears were filled with its rattle and rumble, the beating of horse hooves upon the road no different than the beating of my heart, which thumped so it felt as if it would spring from my chest.

"Stop! Stop!" I shouted, my sole desire not to be run over.

It kept coming.

"Stop! Stop!" I screamed as loudly as I ever screamed before, waving my arms frantically, and jumping up and down.

The postilion hauled back on his reins, a look of dismay on his face, even as he cried out some command. The next moment the lead horse seemed to rise up, hooves pawing the air. The carriage creaked, squeaked, groaned, and swayed as if drunk and then . . . stopped.

"Are you mad, boy?" screamed the coach driver. "What is the matter?" In his hands he had a blunderbuss. It was not, happily, aimed at me.

That was the precise moment when the four masked men stepped out from their hiding places, their many pistols leveled at the coach.

It was the captain who called out: "Throw down your gun or you are dead men all!"

Taken by surprise, the coach driver looked about, then threw his gun down to the road where it lay, quite useless.

As for the postilion, I was surprised to recognize him as Mr. Bartholomew's manservant, he with the grand mustache. As he brushed the dust from his fine livery, he looked down at me with contempt, as if I, a mere boy, had insulted him for stopping the coach.

The captain called out again: "Tell your passengers to step upon the road."

"Out! Out!" cried the coachman. "We have been waylaid!"

For a moment nothing occurred. Even the postilion looked round to see what was happening. Then the stage door swung open wide and out of the coach stepped Mr. Bartholomew.

CHAPTER THIRTY-SEVEN

In Which I Am Party to a Robbery.

M r. Bartholomew!

I had no expectations of seeing any particular person emerge from the stagecoach, but surely Mr. Bartholomew was absolutely the furthest from my mind. I was struck dumb, which means "mute, silent, incapable of speech."

The customs master was not in any way different than when I had last seen him outside the guild hall in Melcombe. I trust I described him properly: a large man with a rough and rosy face, with thick black eyebrows, swept up—I supposed—to make him appear more forceful. He wore the same shoulder-length gooseberry wig. One hand held his tricorn hat. I did note that he did not have his short sword. But he did have his ivory-capped walking stick. In other words, nothing by which to defend himself.

When he stepped out of the coach he did so without the slightest sign of fear. He might have been strolling out of the customs house, the place he did his business. That is, he showed no sign of discomfort—until he turned about and observed me.

When Mr. Bartholomew did see me—please recall that among the highwaymen, I alone was without a mask—his reaction was as severe as mine. He stared at me stupidly, his mouth agape, eyes wide, as if he could not accommodate the image of me where I was. In fact, his body fairly reeled so that his very fine, ivory-capped walking stick, on which he was leaning heavily, snapped in two. He almost fell.

Recovering, the first thing he said was, "Why is this boy here?" Even more amazing, he asked this of the captain. It was almost as if to say, Why have you brought this boy here?

"Why do you ask, sir?" said the captain. "Might you know him?" I could have sworn I detected a sly smirk.

The customs master drew himself up in haughty fashion. "Know him?" he returned in a voice stuffed with sneering. "Of course not!"

Though I knew altogether otherwise, you may be sure I did not speak.

Then abruptly, the customs master was brought back

to the affair at hand, when the captain barked, "Bring out all your money, sir!"

Mr. Bartholomew seemed to need a few moments to compose himself—first by standing somewhat taller, and second by saying in that pompous way he had, as if proclaiming profound laws from a pinnacle, "Sir, I presume you don't know who I am."

I thought this was a marvelous strange statement, since I had seen him in close conversation with Captain Hawkes in Melcombe. To see them face-to-face again brought back a forceful remembrance of that moment. They must know each other very well. My guess that it was Mr. Bartholomew who had informed him about me seemed proven.

"I don't care who you are," said the captain, another outlandish statement.

"I am Weymouth-Melcombe's customs master," returned Mr. Bartholomew with a bow, "an officer of His Majesty, George the First."

"Just bring out your money, sir, and no one will be harmed."

"May I inform you, sir, the money I have with me is customs revenue. It belongs to the king. I am carrying it to London."

He spoke in just that unnatural way, as if he had taken

his words from a script and was repeating his lines, bad acting though it was.

"Bring out the money, sir," repeated the captain.

"If you take it, it will be a most serious crime," proclaimed Mr. Bartholomew.

"Bring it out, sir," the captain prompted, but not, I noted with any anger, urgency, or violence.

Mr. Bartholomew made no forceful resistance of any kind. Instead, he simply turned and looked into the coach. "Bring out the chest," he said. He might as well have said, "Bring out the bread."

He also exchanged a quick glance with his manservant, his postilion, which I decided was a knowing look.

Two men came out of the stagecoach lugging an iron strapped chest, which was closed with a large lock. They looked at the highwaymen. They looked at Mr. Bartholomew.

The customs master said, "Place it on the road."

The men did so.

The captain said, "Open it."

Mr. Bartholomew quickly drew out a key—he must have had it close at hand to be so fast—and unlocked the chest.

Kneeling, the captain threw back the top, looked in, grinned, and then stood up. "You may go, sir," he said.

At that, Mr. Bartholomew looked toward the coachman

who was peering down at all this. "Coachman!" he cried, "I call upon you to witness that I have been robbed by this armed highwayman!"

What else could the coachman say but, "Yes, sir. You have been."

Mr. Bartholomew turned back to the captain. "Thank you, sir."

"I thank you, sir," returned the captain most civilly.

With that, Mr. Bartholomew gave a courtly bow—returned by Captain Hawkes—before climbing back into the coach. His two servants followed.

The captain slammed the coach door shut, and shouted, "Go!"

At that moment the postilion—Mr. Bartholomew's manservant—jumped off his horse and gathered up his master's elegant walking stick—now in two parts—giving me a particularly scornful look while doing so, as if it was I who had broken it. He then remounted, and the whole equipage clattered off.

I, of course, stood off to one side, witnessing all of this. The only moment of distress came when Mr. Bartholomew saw me. Yet once he had seen me and asked his question, he never looked at me again. In fact, it seemed as if he took pains not to consider me again. It was only his manservant, who made it clear he knew me and did so with contempt.

Once the stagecoach had clattered off, the captain and the other highwaymen took no notice of anything but the chest. Captain Hawkes kneeled and then dug his hands among bright silver coins. Laughing, he clearly took great pleasure in feeling the metal. As for his men, there was just as much hilarity.

"That was easy," said one of them.

If anything, it was too easy. I was convinced that the captain and Mr. Bartholomew had planned the entire robbery beforehand.

CHAPTER THIRTY-EIGHT

In Which I Begin to Perceive My Future.

The captain scooped the money into bags and attached the bags to his horse. He also gave handfuls of coins to each of his men. It was a small portion of the whole.

Then he turned to me and said, "Do you want your share?"

Not wishing to incriminate myself any more than I had been forced to, I shook my head.

There was a quick discussion as to how the gang would disperse, and when they might meet again. The time agreed was after, or so I understood, the captain's business in London was completed.

Thereafter, the three men left quickly, leaving me alone with the captain. "Now," he said, "you and I to London."

I did not resist. In the first place, I did not think I could. Second, London was where I wished to go. Once I was there I could put my mind and legs to an escape so as to find my father and sister.

The captain hauled me up as before, took off his mask, and we set off at a canter.

The empty money chest was left behind.

"Why do you think that man asked about you?" the captain said once we had gone along for a while.

"I have no idea," I lied blithely. "He said he came from Melcombe. Perhaps he saw me about town."

"Do you know," the captain said casually, "I think that's not quite true."

"Sir?" I said, feeling some embarrassment for having been caught in my lie.

"I was in Melcombe a few days ago," said the captain. "I met with Mr. Bartholomew."

"Did you?" I said, trying to sound naïve, though as you, my reader, know, I was not surprised to hear this.

"He mentioned a boy and described him rather like you. He said you stole money from a wreck that was cast ashore during the recent storm. Told me the exact amount. Twenty-three shillings. Money you did not deny taking. He informed me that he wished to hold you so as to bring your lawyer father in. It appears he wishes to lay a charge against your parent for fraud. When you came into the Swan Inn the other night I recognized you right away."

"Did you, sir?" I said, rather weakly.

He laughed. "Of course."

"Sir, why would Mr. Bartholomew tell you about me?"

"We have a good friend in common."

"Who would that be, sir?"

"Jonathan Wild."

"Mr. Wild? The thief?"

The captain laughed and said, "The thief-catcher."

"Is Mr. Bartholomew a . . . thief?"

"If Mr. Wild lodges information against him, he will be. Of that, you can be a witness. But mind, Mr. Bartholomew can be a witness against you as well."

"For what?"

"For waylaying the stage."

It was then and there I learned a major lesson. To wit: when we do wrong we bind ourselves to other people who do wrong. Moreover, it was the captain who was spreading the glue. He had arranged everything so that Mr. Bartholomew and I would be mutually tied together in crime.

To test this maxim, I said to the captain: "And London, sir, why are you going there?"

"I need to bring Mr. Wild this money. The money you and I just stole."

"Me, sir?" I said weakly.

"You stopped the stagecoach, did you not?"

"Mr. Bartholomew seemed willing enough to give you the money."

"To be sure. He'll get back his share. Oliver, it is the way of the world."

"I don't wish to think so, sir."

"You are young!" he exclaimed.

I said no more. Instead, I pondered how these men were all connected: Mr. Bartholomew, Mr. Sandys, Captain Hawkes, Mr. Wild, and . . . me.

Had I—who until recently had lived a moral life of little worry—had I a truly become a criminal?

I had to admit, it seemed so.

CHAPTER THIRTY-NINE

In Which I First See London.

Our journey to London took three days. Early on, Captain Hawkes purchased a horse for me—an old piebald mare—good enough to have me mount, which—I admit—pleased me. He also made me promise I would not ride off. I intended to keep my word, since London was the place I wished to go and being horsed made my journey only easier. Besides, since I did not know how to ride, I could not steal away from the captain, the much superior horseman. In any case, he spent much time in instructing me as we went along.

As we covered the miles, Captain Hawkes entertained me with many a tale about his life and adventures. He came—he said—from a well-turned family, his father being a country parson. He was given what he called a "liberal education" so as to make him a gentleman with high hopes for marrying well, and living on an estate in the country. Then his father passed away, and his estate proved to be far less than promised.

"Was I to become a drudge?" the captain asked me. "A laboring man? An apprentice in a shop?"

His voice was so full of scorn his answer was obviously no. I had learned that when adults ask that kind of question of the young, they do not want your answer, but merely ask so they might give you their own response.

"I knew how to use a pistol," he went on. "I knew politeness. I was excellent with horses. I could talk with gentlemen. And," he added, "I had brains. If that is not the perfect description of a highwayman, I know not otherwise.

"I live well in London; the best society. What is virtuous society?" he said with a laugh. "A community, in which, when a bill is paid, you don't ask from where the money comes."

Then he told me of his adventures as a highwayman, which had much to do with sword fights, men he had slain, clever tricks he had played, and, yes, the many thefts he had managed to bring off.

All quite dreadful, but engaging.

Since the young are rarely offered friendship from an adult, I was flattered by his companionship. As he talked, and the hours passed, I stopped thinking of him as a lawless highwayman, but accepted him as an adventurous fellow full of engaging stories. I listened with interest, and without disapproval.

Was this his wicked design?

He asked little about me, and in any case, I was careful not to say much. I did tell him about my father and my deceased mother, but not a word about my sister, Charity. When he asked me why Father had gone to London, I simply said, which was true enough, it was some business of which I knew little, but that—here I did lie—he had asked me to join him.

"Are you," asked the captain, "going to warn him about Mr. Bartholomew's charges against him?"

"Do you think I should?" I asked, pretending innocence.

"It might be wise. Bartholomew is a spiteful fellow who thinks overmuch of himself."

I could agree with that.

Along the way we stopped at inns, where the captain fed me well. I offered to pay from my small stock of shillings—still in my pocket—but he insisted upon covering the charge.

"If you are to have any pleasure in London, you'll need every penny you have."

No doubt that was why when alone I studied my coins with care, coming to know them individually—as friends—such as the one that had a scratch upon its silver face.

During evening meals the captain pushed me aside and played cards or backgammon with any who chose to play. He generally did well but unlike Father, he was not always a winner. Moreover, he paid his debts on demand. All in all, he was in such good cheer everyone liked him. His primary mask was his engaging smile. As for what he intended for me in London I did not ask. My intent was that once there I would slip away.

After a number of days we approached London.

It was my sister who had told me that the population of Melcombe was about four thousand. Father had said the number of people residing in London was five hundred thousand.

Both were right.

I shall never forget my first view of the city. We had ridden along the road, up some hill, and when we reached its summit, I looked out over the entire city of London. It was colossal. The stars in Heaven numbered fewer than the quantity of buildings I saw. These buildings were punctuated by the spires of many churches, the biggest—as I would learn—being the great dome of St. Paul's.

At that distance a dull gray cloud hovered over the city. Even from afar, I could smell it, strong and foul, a stench not unlike an old washing cloth that had been used to clean a mess, and then allowed to rot.

Though London seemed to be a congealed mass of things hard to distinguish one from the other, as we entered the city proper, that solid bulk fell asunder into uncountable and incomprehensible bits.

To begin, the sheer number of people astonished me: crowds of crowds. I could not have imagined that the whole world contained as many people as did London. Yet here they were, pressed together like limitless seeds in a colossal bin.

People old and young, men, women, children, all walking, running, riding, selling, being carried, standing about, or staggering. Beggars—mostly women—prodigious in number and begging everywhere. Upon the streets people asleep, or dead, sniffed by rats or dogs.

Individuals dressed in every fashion imaginable, a chaos of color, a rainbow gone mad, hues I could not begin to name.

The great majority of folk appeared poor, but many were clearly wealthy. People wrapped in rags as well as those sumptuously dressed in what seemed to be silks and furs. Yet all these different levels of people mingled.

The richer sort, men and women, wore wigs, trailing what appeared to be clouds of powder. The poorer had no wigs. But as I would learn, head lice were everywhere.

There were buildings upon buildings, pushed together, crushed together, squeezed together, many leaning over the streets, so close to one another one might leap from roof to roof. As we passed down one street I saw a building collapse in a cloud of debris, people fleeing, people watching, a few cheering, but apparently not that extraordinary as it was to me.

Mazes of narrow streets bent and twisted now this direction, now that, filled to their boundaries with garbage, filth fairly flowing down center gutters. Mud and dust everywhere. Within the city, the smell I had noted from afar was much intensified—dung, offal, rotting food, dead animals, rats, cats and dogs. It was truly sickening to me, who had lived my life by the fresh and open sea.

Countless wagons, carts, carriages, and sedan chairs. Teams of horses, herds of cattle, packs of dogs, a great swirling menagerie of baying, yowling, and barking creatures.

Unending numbers of shops with their classifying signs thrust over streets. Every seventh building seemingly a drinking place, for coffee, beer, or gin. Vast numbers of people staggering, in varied degrees of intoxication.

And the noise! A constant drumming of jabber, buzzes, chatter, shouts, and screams, as if the half million people living there were forever talking at one and the same time. Midst them, musicians making music along with the cries of endless vendors. Church bells trying to sing over the din.

I had to wonder if any listened, could listen.

"Monstrous," my father had called London and yes,

to my eyes it was a monster with multiple heads, hands, and legs.

If all this seems no more than a list, I confess I experienced it that way, for what I witnessed was an unboundedness of things, which I noted with little comprehension.

In all this hurly-burly the captain was calm, and as far as I could tell, undaunted by what so overwhelmed me. Where I was instantly, totally disordered, seeing no pattern to anything, he seemed to know exactly where he was going as we made our way through the throngs.

I kept turning this way and that, my mind desperately trying to name objects, as if to fasten them to my thoughts, so as to understand things, guess things, struggling to make sense of it all! It was baffling, frightening, enthralling all at once.

And then, in the midst of all these things and all these people, I thought I saw Father.

CHAPTER FORTY

A Brief Chapter Which Tells You How I Came to Fully Understand My Predicament.

I do not know if it is true for you, but for me, to see something I do know in the midst of the confusion of what I don't know is a shock. I blink to see what I think I've seen—sure I have seen it—only to have it vanish the next moment. It's rather like the foam frothing upon a rolling wave. Surely it is there, but in moments it disappears, submerged in the greater sea. So I had to wonder if I truly had seen my father.

Allowing myself to think I had seen him, I cried out, "Father!" But for all the noise, voices, and murmurs cascading about, I might as well have been shouting into my hat.

No doubt, too, there were many fathers near where I

was horsed. Indeed, two men actually looked about, but they were nobody I knew.

Had I seen him? I surely wished to. But then, I've come to believe that nothing brings on seeing a thing as wanting to see it.

Not that I could constrain myself. "Captain!" I cried. "It's my father!"

He turned in his saddle. "Where?"

"There!" I returned, pointing in the general direction I thought I'd seen him go. The next moment I leaped off my horse and tried to drive my way through the crowds. It was like forcing myself through a pile of loose bricks. People pushed back from all directions, buffeting me so that I made but little progress. Keep in mind that my height—not great—prevented me from seeing much of where I was going.

A strong hand came down upon my shoulder. I whirled about. It was the captain. "Show me and I'll fetch him."

It was a simple, reasonable request, but impossible to do. All the unexpected events that happened to me from the time I discovered Father had gone from Melcombe to this moment, when I thought I had seen him, gathered in my chest like a ball of hot lead. It was hard to breathe.

Had I seen him? In truth, I think not.

Had I wanted to see him? I did.

The weight of my loneliness—missing my sister, my father, and my home in Melcombe—fell upon me. I had been swept away, buffeted, stolen, captured, and kidnapped—call it what you will—by a slew of scoundrels, and twisted into a thief.

The captain was looking down at me with sympathy, even kindness, but as I looked up at him I had but one emotion: I hated him.

I must get free! I told myself. Somewhere in this monstrous city is my sister. She will protect me, save me. I must find her!

Not wishing to acknowledge my folly, I merely said, "He's gone," and felt defeated.

"You'll gain a better view from the horses," he said. He led me back to them, picked me up bodily, and set me on the saddle. He, too, mounted.

"Look about. Do you see him?"

Gazing over the hordes of people I saw no hint of Father.

"He's . . . gone," I managed to say. "I don't know where." Then, with distress, I admitted, "I'm not even sure it was him."

The captain stood high in his saddle and looked about as if he might spy him out, but of course he had no idea what he looked like.

I suddenly wanted to tell the captain everything that

had happened, my father's disappearance for reasons I did not know, my desire to find him and even more, my sister, Charity. I held back, fearful of telling him too much, not wishing to be any more entangled with him than I already was. Though for the most part he acted kindly, I reminded myself he was a highwayman, that he had kidnapped me for some purpose of his own.

Ashamed of my confused emotions and thoughts, I dried my face and sat there looking round at the crowds of people. It was of no use. If I had seen my father, he had gone. I knew not where. But all in all, I gave myself this flutter of hope: Father was in this vast city, somewhere. More vitally, so was my sister.

Captain Hawkes bestowed a sympathetic smile and patted my arm. "Let's believe it was him," he said. "That way we have every reason to think we can find him. Now, stay close."

I followed mutely, but then my horse was still tethered to his, so I had little choice. As I gazed upon the multitude of people I had eyes only for what I did not see, my sister.

CHAPTER FORTY-ONE

In Which I Discover a Loss, but Perhaps a Gain.

The captain led me to his home. At first sight I was taken aback by its size and apparent wealth, but the captain assured me he lived only in a top-floor garret.

We got off our horses and removed the captain's heavy saddle bags, which were full of money and that gold snuffbox. Then we turned to the house.

The house itself was red brick, four stories high, including top garrets with many windows, or rather places for windows, for the government counted windows so as to calculate a building tax. As a result, some windows were covered over, and sat upon the face of the building like sleeping eyes.

Behind an iron fence, we stepped up a few stone steps to the front door, next to which, on the ground, was a bar of iron. The captain explained the bar was meant for scraping London mud from the soles of boots. London had much in excess but perhaps mud was what it manufactured most.

The door opened and a boy stepped out. "Put these horses in the stable," the captain said to him, giving him a small coin. To me, he said, "Come along."

The small coin was my introduction to a fundamental London fact: One paid for everything, even courtesy.

Inside the building was a flight of stairs that went up and around floor by floor until it reached the top. As we progressed, the captain informed me who lived in each area. "They think of me as a charming young gentleman of independent means."

For my part I was disliking him more and more.

When we reached the highest level, he unlocked two stout locks that kept a door closed. "My London home," he announced as we stepped inside.

It was far less splendid than all his talk of wealth and success had led me to believe. The one room had an empty fireplace on the left-side wall, with an artistic print fastened over the mantel. On the right wall, a freestanding closet. Three chairs, a small table (on which stood a bottle of ink, quills, and paper). Where the roof slanted sharply down, a bed built into the wall. Such was the furniture.

Over the bed was a small window plus a narrow shelf that held three leather-bound books. I recall a small cupboard attached to a wall. The floor was bare. There was no more.

He pointed to one of the chairs and said, "You may sit there."

As I did, he set his bags of money on the table, poured out the coins, and began to stack them on the table. "In business," he said to me over his shoulder, "accounting is the thing. If you don't know what money you have, you might as well have nothing."

I sat still, my mind in a whirl about thinking I'd seen Father, trying to plan how I might escape and search for him. I had some money. To reassure myself I put my hand in my pocket. That crumpled letter from my father was there. As for the coins, they were not there.

"My money is gone!" I cried out.

"Where had you put it?"

"My trouser pocket."

"The worst place," he admonished. "When you went into the crowd," he said, "a shoulder sham must have taken it." He showed no surprise but merely stated this as an ordinary occurrence.

"What's . . . a shoulder sham?" I asked.

"A pickpocket. These knuckle wipes, as some call them, are everywhere. Highly skilled, too. Boys and girls, for the most part. Rather like you," he added with a smile.

"I felt nothing," I protested.

"I'll need to teach you some security, how to notice when you're being plucked."

With those casual words he turned back to his accounting.

For me it was yet another catastrophe. Now I had no money by which to gain my independence. I stood beside Hawkes watching him count and stack his coins. This is when I suddenly observed that shilling with a scratch across its face: my shilling.

It was none other than the captain who had picked my pocket! And he had done it so he might increase my dependency.

Even so, I felt powerless to say or do anything.

Instead, I wandered around the room, as if I were in a cage. At one point I paused to look at the print that was over the fireplace. It depicted a handsome young man, dressed in high fashion. Next to him an old, ugly woman. They were holding hands. She was smiling. He looked grim. A minister stood before them. Beneath the print were the words:

Married for Money!!!

I supposed it was meant to be humorous. The faces of the man and woman were highly animated.

I looked at the words again, "Married for Money." As I

did I felt a sudden prickle in my brain. I yanked my father's letter from my pocket and looked at what was written:

Charity XX XXXXX XX be mXXXXXd!!

Only then did I finally grasp what the smeared letters meant: Charity was planning to be married! Or had already done so.

My shock was great, but at least it enabled me to understand why Father had dashed to London so suddenly. Charity married! It would be the last thing he would have allowed her to do.

As I was trying to make sense of my discovery, the captain said, "There. Everything tabulated." He sanded the wet ink so it would not smudge—the way my father's letter had smudged. Then he held his paper up to the light and read over what he had written. "Now we have to bring this information to the man who will decide what to do with it. And the quantity of money I received must be reported to Mr. Wild. At the King's Head Inn."

Mr. Wild! The man so many had spoken about with awe and dread. The name jolted me from my thoughts about Charity and Father. "Must I see him?"

"You must."

"Do we bring all that money to him?" I asked.

Captain Hawkes laughed. "That's the genius of the man. He never touches a penny. He's only a thief-catcher."

"What thieves does he catch?"

"Anyone he chooses to catch. He knows every criminal in Great Britain and Ireland. He can make and break them all."

A new and terrible thought came to me: I had become a thief. Did that mean that this Mr. Wild would break me?

CHAPTER FORTY-TWO

In Which I Learn More about Mr. Jonathan Wild, Chief Thief-Taker of Great Britain and Ireland

The captain closed the door to his room with his double locks, and once below we began to walk through narrow streets. These streets twisted and turned as if in a maze, although all the people around me seemed to know where they were going, and moved with ease. It seemed as if only I was befuddled.

"Please, sir," I asked as we went along, "why must I see this Mr. Wild?"

"He will decide what to do with you."

"But . . . what might he decide?"

"He has a genius for invention. I never try to predict him. Every thief in Great Britain is employed by him. Anything such thieves take—money or objects—is shared with Mr. Wild, and thereby gains his protection. Once a thing is stolen, Mr. Wild offers it back to the victim for a price. Or he sells it, in this country or France.

"If Mr. Wild does not like what a thief does, if they do not obey his commands, or act without his permission, they—like Mr. Sandys—are turned over to the magistrates and judges, and Mr. Wild provides evidence against them. Such a one is doomed. Never forget that."

"Does everyone know he acts this way?" I asked. "Even the victims?"

"If they don't they are fools. You do not go against Mr. Wild. But don't worry. He'll find you a place soon enough."

I shuddered. The captain must have sensed my unease, for though he said no more, he kept his hand lightly on my shoulder. If he had meant to reassure me, it did the opposite.

The sign that proclaimed the King's Head Inn was a painted portrait of a glaring king—just his head—wearing a crown. His name, "Charles I," was written under it. It caused me to recall the name Mr. Probert had given me—"Charles"—because Oliver Cromwell had—so the schoolmaster claimed—removed this king's head. And here it was, an image of that head, swinging outside a tavern.

The sign hung over a wide door, through which poured a great throng of people, mostly men. Inside, the inn proved to be a dimly lit and smoky place with candles in wall sconces, the air rank with the stench of gin and beer, tobacco smoke and sweat.

The candlelight barely illuminated the scene. There was a serving bar against one wall and on the opposite wall, a fireplace, with smoky coals. There were tables and chairs aplenty, occupied by people constantly talking, which filled the room with chatter. While there was much drinking, too, many were reading newspapers or pamphlets. Others were playing cards or tossing dice. I even saw a table with a backgammon board, which put to mind my father's gambling. For a moment I felt my life consisted of nothing but inns and outs.

But as I looked around I was startled to see none other than Mr. Bartholomew in a far corner intent upon reading a paper.

I plucked on the captain's sleeve. "Sir, I think Mr.—"

"We need to hurry," he said, cutting me off.

Captain Hawkes guided me forward, making his way through the crowded room, nodding to this one, now that one. I stole a look back. Mr. Bartholomew was no longer there. Had he seen me and fled? I wondered. What if he was reporting me to some magistrate, and charging me with being a highwayman?

The captain was intent on moving toward the far back of the room, where there was a table near a partly open door as if for easy exit.

Seated behind the table was a short, stocky man, with broad shoulders and a bulky black coat. His heavy, scowling, poorly shaved face bore thick lips, a large, beakish nose, and slightly bulging eyes beneath dark eyebrows. His hat had been pulled low over a short brown wig. His coat was partly open, and sticking out of it—as though meant to be seen—was the butt end of a pistol.

As we approached him, a woman, who had been standing there talking to him, turned around. Tall and better dressed than the other women in the tavern, she had a long and narrow face and a double chin, and bore a look of disdain. Her black hair, tied behind her head, was topped by a cap from which two white ribbons dangled. Her skirt was full and she had a short apron. When she went by us, she did not deign to look to the left or the right, certainly not at us.

The captain paid her no mind either, but as he and I went forward, I observed the man at the table working his way through a small book. He was turning the pages over, one by one, touching a finger to his pink tongue before moving on to a new leaf, the protruding tongue suggestive of a snake. Now and again he made a mark in the book with a quill pen.

When we came up to the table, the captain halted and said, "Mr. Wild, sir. Captain Hawkes at your service."

I was standing before the man Mr. Sandys had called "the devil's own serpent."

CHAPTER FORTY-THREE

In Which Mr. Jonathan Wild Decides What to Do with Me.

M r. Wild scowled, put down his book and pen, and folded his large stubby-fingered hands before him, then looked up at me. Though he said nothing, his look contained a combination of judgment, threat, and a frightful force that alarmed me much.

"Mr. Sandys has been warned," said the captain, as if delivering a report. "And Mr. Bartholomew has delivered."

"To what degree?"

"One hundred and thirty pounds. And there was a stagecoach; fifteen pounds plus a gold snuffbox. A Mr. John Kolbert seems to have lost it."

Knowing exactly how the captain stole that snuffbox I wondered at the word "lost."

Mr. Wild made a brusque nod and said, "A notice will

be posted. And who is this boy?" All along he had kept his malevolent gaze on me.

"Isn't he the perfect shoulder sham?" said the captain, with a tuck of his hand beneath my chin to draw my face up. "Have you ever seen more innocence?"

Mr. Wild's emotion while looking at me was no more expressive than a lump of ice. "It's always better," he said, "when they start young. But he'll be better with smarter clothing."

"Easily done."

"Then you may do so," said Mr. Wild. "What's his name?"

"Oliver Pitts."

Mr. Wild picked up his little book, dipped his quill into his pot of ink, and scratched in my name. The moment he did so I recalled Mr. Sandys's words: "If he puts your name in his book, you belong to him."

Mr. Wild blew on the writing to dry the ink and glanced up again. "He will be under your charge, Captain. Use him well." It was a dismissal.

What reechoed in my mind was the word "use."

The captain put his hand on my shoulder, turned me about—I was so distressed I had lost the power of movement—and guided me back toward the entry door. Halfway there, he paused and said, "Come here."

He led me to a table around which sat four people,

three men and a woman. "Gentlemen. My dear," he said, giving a bow.

They exchanged nods plus words of rough and vulgar greeting, after which the captain brought me forward. "My new shoulder sham."

All four studied me with what I took to be amusement. One of the men said, "Right out of the choir, isn't he?"

They all laughed.

"I intend," said the captain, "to try him tomorrow eve at Covent Garden. Shall we say seven o'clock sharp?"

"All's game with us," said the woman.

Though no more was said, they seemed to have a full understanding among themselves because the captain—without another word—led me out of the King's Head. As we passed onto the street, I glanced up at the sign: the scowling head of the decapitated king seemed the very image of Mr. Wild.

I only wished it was.

As the captain and I went along I said, "Please, sir, why did you refer to me as a shoulder sham?"

"Do you like the thought of thieves?" he answered.

"No, sir."

"Though you are one yourself."

"I didn't mean to be," I said meekly.

"Well then, would you like to make the world safer from thieves?"

"Yes, sir, I suppose I would."

"Excellent! Mr. Wild is giving you that opportunity. It's all quite simple. Tomorrow you will be at Covent Garden. You will be dressed well, appearing as young, innocent, and rich. You will have a silk handkerchief poking out of your pocket. It being Covent Garden, you can be sure someone will try to pick that pocket."

Knowing who had picked my pocket, I glanced at him with suspicion. "The way I lost my money?"

"Precisely. Except now you will be a lure. The pickpocket will spy your handkerchief. He will move with stealth behind your back so you won't see him. When he tugs upon your handkerchief you will drop your hand, catch the thief by the wrist, hold him, and give the hue and cry: 'Thief! Thief!'

"Of course, I shall instruct you how to know when they try to take your handkerchief.

"Now then, my four friends—you just met them—will be near. Upon hearing your cry they will lay hands on the thief and hold him. Directly, you shall carry him—with my friends—to a magistrate. The thief will be charged. Sent to gaol. Found guilty. You will be awarded forty pounds sterling for catching and convicting a thief. That money—most of it of course—goes to Mr. Wild."

"Please, sir," I said after a moment, "what happens to the thief?"

The captain laughed. "Depending on judge and jury, he will be whipped, branded, placed in a pillory, hanged, or transported to the colonies."

Shocked, I looked up at the captain. "Sir," I said, "will I be in any danger?"

"Not a speck."

"Where will you be when this happens?"

"Looking on from a safe distance."

"Close?"

"Close enough to make sure you do as you're told. Now come along," he said, "we must fit you with some better clothing to play the part."

Upon hearing such a plan—and my role—I felt embarrassment and dismay that I should be used in such a fashion. But as I reviewed what the captain proposed to do, I saw a clear opportunity. That is to say, I would do precisely what he told me to do. A thief would come and pull upon the handkerchief. I'd catch him. "Thief!" I'd call as instructed. Captain Hawkes's four rogues would close in to secure the thief.

At that moment—as the captain's accomplices worked to hold the pickpocket, and surely the thief must struggle to get away—they would be intent on him, not me. That moment would be my best chance of escape. I need only to plunge into the nearest, thickest crowd, and become lost to their sight. I would be free. Where I might eventually go was a whole other question.

Elated at my cleverness, I swore to myself I would absolutely do just that. For the first time in a goodly while my spirits soared.

CHAPTER FORTY-FOUR

In Which I Work Toward My Escape.

The captain took me to a tailor's shop along some back street. There, an old, stooped man with small eyes and spidery fingers fitted me with a fine blue jacket with wide sleeves, silver-looking buttons, and huge pockets. The captain directed that a silk handkerchief be inserted into my right-side pocket and had the tailor sew that handkerchief tightly to the bottom of the pocket. In other words, the handkerchief could not be withdrawn. If any effort was made to remove it, it would pull and most assuredly I'd feel it. Sensing the tug, I would turn and thereby catch the thief.

I took pains to admire the plan, the more so since I was convinced it would allow me to escape.

The clothing once paid for, we returned to the captain's

room and for a good part of the remaining day we practiced how I would catch the shoulder sham. The captain had me stand in the middle of the room, facing now this way, now that. He would then sidle up to me and with light-fingered dexterity tease out the silk handkerchief. Because of the way it was secured, I always felt the tug. At that precise moment I'd bring my right hand down sharply, clutch the captain's wrist, and hold it tight.

"Excellent!" proclaimed the captain after some diligent hours of work. "You will make your fortune in catching thieves and winning rewards." How pleased he was with his plan. But, oh, how delighted I was with the cleverness of my plan, altogether certain that he had no idea what I intended to do.

That evening the captain locked me in his room and went out upon the town, I know not where. I did not ask. I was glad to be alone. Though I doubted the likelihood of success, I tried to open the locked door. Not possible. I attempted the window with equal failure. I could do nothing but remain.

Instead, I returned to a study of my father's letter. That Charity was about to be married, or already was married, continued to astound me. Who was the man? How had she met him? Would I like him? Would he like me? Would Charity and I still be the best of friends? Of course, I was aware that none of that mattered unless I could find her. And I would not be able to find her unless I first gained my freedom.

Eventually, I fell asleep and did not wake till morning. When I arose, I found that the captain had returned and now it was he who slept. Bored, I went through the pages of *Parker's London Weekly*, which he must have purchased the previous eve, finding it mildly entertaining with its London news and gossip. Then I came upon this advertisement:

> Stolen out of the hands of Mr. John Kolbert, esquire, along the Dorchester Road: a gold snuffbox. If any person concerned in the said robbery will discover his accomplices, so that they may be brought to justice, apply to Mr. Jonathan Wild at the King's Head in the Old Bailey, and he shall have Ten Pounds reward.

But right there on Captain Hawkes's table was Mr. John Kolbert's gold snuffbox. All this informed me precisely how Mr. Wild worked: Captain Hawkes, having stolen the snuffbox from Mr. Kolbert, was now holding it until Mr. Wild could sell it back to the victim. Mr. Kolbert, presumably, would see the advertisement and bring ten pounds to Wild, thereby buying back what was stolen from him. Wild was indeed a wicked man, as was Captain Hawkes.

All of which is to say I was well aware I was standing on a precipice; if I failed to make my escape, I would not likely have another chance. Before the day was done I would either be free or forever locked into a life of crime.

Or a prison.

CHAPTER FORTY-FIVE

The Momentous Chapter in Which a Shoulder Sham Picks My Pocket.

It was late afternoon when the captain took me—dressed in my fine new blue jacket—to Covent Garden. I hardly knew what to expect of such a place, save that I assumed it must be a garden. It proved to be nothing of the sort. Rather, it was a large square surrounded by many buildings, including at least one church. In fact, it proved to be an extensive market for the selling of corn, vegetables, flowers, and herbs. Many dealers simply spread their goods upon the pavement. Others had stalls. Any number walked about and cried their goods. I saw one man with a tower of hats upon his head, which he offered for sale.

Buyers were great in numbers, too, on foot, on horses, in carriages and sedan chairs. Many of the people were quite ordinary, but I saw the wealthy, too. Beyond all else, like so much of what I had seen of London, the market was a mass of people.

"Now," the captain said to me when we had reached the middle of the market surrounded by many, "all you need to do is wander about as if you've nothing to do than be idle. I promise you, someone will try to take the handkerchief." He teased the silk handkerchief from my pocket so that it hung partly out. "Mind," he said, giving me his best smile, "there will be eyes on you."

I recalled the fishermen of Melcombe, who tied bits of food to a string and threw it into the sea, in hopes a large fish would bite into it. If one did, the fisherman would pull the hapless creature to shore and in time devoured it. This was much the same case: I had been turned into bait. The big difference was that both I and the one I caught would be devoured. My sole hope was that my catch would put up a long struggle. To my shame, let it be admitted I cared little for his fate, being concerned only with mine.

"What about your friends?" I asked.

"I assure you," said the captain, "they are here, and are prepared."

"Are you certain?"

"I am. We shall catch the thief and shall share the reward, including you. Now go, and remember all we have practiced."

He placed a hand on my shoulder. "I congratulate you. You are on your way to a wealthy and successful life."

As I looked up at him, and his smile, my heart suddenly misgave me. Had he some other plan in mind, something to do me harm? Some measure I had not considered? Should I run off now?

All of which is to say, I was utterly agitated. For if his companions were watching me—and the captain said they were—I would be quickly recaptured, and I had no doubt things would go badly. I had seen what happened to Mr. Sandys.

Before I could steady my mind, Captain Hawkes gave me a little shove, as if pushing a small boat upon the waters of the wide sea. Heart pounding, I went forward only to pause for a moment and glance back at the captain. He nodded, while offering his most engaging smile. Deciding it would be wisest to follow my original plan, I moved on and aimed for the thickest of crowds. Mind, I was short, so it felt as if all of humanity was towering in and about me.

Anticipating I knew not what, I walked about slowly, waiting for something to happen. My stomach churned.

Then, before I knew it, I felt a tug.

Perfectly practiced, I dropped my right hand down, felt a narrow wrist, gripped it as tightly as I could, then spun about and looked up into the thief's face.

It was my sister, Charity.

CHAPTER FORTY-SIX

In Which I Tell You What Followed This Astounding Moment.

For perhaps two seconds Charity and I gawped at each other with simultaneous amazedness.

"Charity!" I exclaimed and if ever an exclamation point was obligatory, it was for that moment.

"Oliver!" she gasped in turn.

It was I who recovered my wits first. Still holding on to Charity's hand, I cried, "Run!" and fairly dragging her, plunged into the densest of crowds. In that instant we were free, but it was as if all the evils of the world were pursuing us.

And they were.

"Thief! Thief!" came cries. "Stop, thief!" rang round us like a ragged choir.

I had no doubt it was Captain Hawkes and his four

friends who had given the hue and cry, seeking to enlist others to run us down and hold us. Never mind that real thieves were chasing the innocent, which is to say Charity and me; we ran as if the hounds of hell were at our heels.

I would learn the pursuit of criminals through the streets of London was a citywide sport and entertainment. As we dashed across Covent Garden market square, alarms and howls erupted all round us.

I darted a look back. A mob of people was in full chase, people who knew nothing save there was a bloodlust hunt. No fox was ere pursued by more barking hounds than we.

I was too terrified to think, but Charity saved us. She dropped my hand, stepped slightly away, and faced the mob. "There!" she cried, pointing. "He went there!"

The thrilled crowd veered off in the direction she indicated.

As the people rushed by, Charity again took up my hand and led the way, walking fast—not running, lest we attract attention—toward Southampton Street. Even though we reached it, and no longer were being chased, she continued, not talking, but striding purposefully on, until we came to the wide street known as the Strand.

As you well know by now, I had had many adventures all on my own. But by freeing us from the mob, in a stroke, Charity reclaimed her protection over me, I more than willing. She led me across a wide street—dodging horses, sedan chairs, coaches as well as many pedestrians—into a narrow alley known as Dirty Lane and shortly after, a sharp left turn onto Crois Court. There we stopped, panting, only then truly looking at each other. To be sure we hugged and hugged again, full of joy that we had found each other.

But then, in turnabout, I suddenly recalled that I had come upon Charity only because she had been attempting to pick my pocket. This is to say I had just discovered that my beloved sister was a thief.

I beg you to consider my state of confusion. To love someone greatly, to absolutely trust and depend on them, only to discover that the same person is dishonest, is an utterly confounding moment. As I looked upon my sister, my emotions moved simultaneously in opposite directions— attraction and revulsion.

The best I could stammer was, "What . . . what happened to you?"

Instead of replying, Charity said, "We need to find a safer place to talk."

I was in too much a muddled state to do anything but follow her commands. Even so, as we went along I kept stealing glances at her. It took no sharp intelligence to observe that much had happened. Though she somehow maintained her neatness, and her dignity, her garments were torn and dirty, her face besmirched. It was as if she was in some coarse costume, but could not fully mask her true self, the one I knew.

Charity led, we rushed on, till we were on the Strand again. Once there we went to a fine church, called, I believe, St. Clements. On its south prospect was a small, domed structure, which had a place obscured by a circle of pillars where we could sit out of sight. Even better, the tumultuous noise and confusion of London seemed to melt away, leaving us in a kind of private sanctuary. Once there we both took deep breaths.

"We can talk here," Charity whispered.

Seated close, our breath recovered, she clutched my right hand and gave it a loving kiss. "I have missed you so much," she said only to shudder. Was the shudder one of relief or shame? The truth is, I was afraid to ask how she came to be as I found her, a pickpocket. I waited.

"Now," she said at last, allowing me to avoid the question I didn't wish to ask, "tell me how you came to London and Covent Garden."

"I came for you, and Father."

"Father?" she cried. "Is he in London? Where?"

As speedily as I could, I informed her about the great storm, the damage to our home, Father's abrupt going to London, Mr. Bartholomew, the poorhouse, and my subsequent decision to leave Melcombe.

"But . . . why did Father come here?"

"I believe he thought you were about to be married and wished to stop you. He left me a letter but it was so damaged in the storm I couldn't read it, making his departure a mystery. At first I was determined to wait for him—so as to warn him about Mr. Bartholomew—but then came my unfortunate stay at the poorhouse, which forced me to flee Melcombe and come to London in hopes of finding you and Father."

I told her how I had fallen in with a Mr. Sandys and then Captain Hawkes; how I stopped the coach, how Hawkes brought me to Mr. Wild who put my name in his book. Then, finally, the plan to trap pickpockets for reward money, by which I planned to escape.

"Does this Captain Hawkes truly work for Mr. Wild?" asked Charity. She was pale enough, but had turned like chalk at the mention of Wild's name.

"He does."

"Oliver, nothing could be more ruinous," she said. "Everyone in London knows Mr. Wild. He's an affrightening man. A terrible criminal. It's commonly said there's no wrongdoing in this entire city or kingdom that is not arranged by him."

"But you," I said, finally having the courage to speak, "why are you here? I thought you went to our uncle's home. Why do you look so poorly? Are you truly . . . a pickpocket?"

As if wanting to hide her shame, she put her hands

over her face. Gently, I pulled her fingers down. "Charity," I said, "I must know."

"Are you sure?"

I nodded.

It took her some moments before she spoke again. I sat there patiently.

"I did go to our uncle's," she began, "thinking it would be a good and comfortable place. But because of my folly, I was forced to come into great misfortune."

"Tell me," I said, hardly knowing which held me most, fascination or fear.

Charity closed her eyes as if her story was too painful to look upon. She opened them, gazed at me with palpable affection, sighed, and began to relate the history of her time in London.

CHAPTER FORTY-SEVEN

In Which I Hear Charity's Story.

You know why I came to London: to gain some independence in life, and have some pleasures before I grew too old. I'll concede I had dreams of finding a seemly husband since Father was not likely to accept any possible suitor I might attract. As you well know, though Father has provided a home and food for us he has given little else. How often have you heard him say, 'I have not been a good parent. I promise to do better.'"

"Many times."

"Our uncle, Tobias Cuttlewaith and his wife, had, by letters, offered me a home, affection, and protection. They suggested their business establishment was large and successful, and that I was welcome to live with them on the familiar terms of a daughter—since they were childless.

"I took the coach to London, where I was received civilly enough by our aunt and uncle. I learned that Uncle's shop on Hanover Street was one that sold and repaired walking sticks for gentlemen. But only when my relations took me in did they inform me they expected me to work for them."

"A lot of work?" I asked.

"I've never been chary of effort. You know how I cared for you and Father, taking pride in my orderliness and cleanness. I would have been happy and willing to do my share for my relations, but they would have it that I should be in their shop every day, all day, early morning till eve. Moreover, since I am pretty, they wished me to play the coquet with their customers, so as to induce them to buy more expensive goods."

"What do you mean, 'play the coquet'?"

She blushed. "To act as if I found gentlemen customers attractive so as to induce them to make a purchase. Oliver, it made me uncomfortable. What had I to do with walking sticks? Promoting them made me feel toadish."

As she spoke my emotions were increasingly peppered: How could they treat my sister so!

"I had my late evenings free, and Sunday mornings as well, though I was expected to go to their church where the sermons were insufferably long. Moreover, our uncle paid me no wages, allowing that my bed and board was all that was due me."

"You were treated so unfairly," I cried.

"And mistreated. Not sure what to do, I chose to bide my time before I did anything. I did have a small amount of Father's money remaining, which I knew I must hoard.

"Alas, you cannot believe how expensive things in London are. As a result, such money as I had soon melted away on trifles till I had very little. Thus I grew completely dependent on our uncle and aunt.

"What was worse, as time went on they used me with growing harshness, treated me as a low servant, threatened to beat me with their canes, spoke coarsely to me. At the same time they left me alone in their shop while they went to pleasure gardens so as to mingle with gentlemen, 'for business,' they said."

"You should have sent for me," I said. "I would have rescued you."

She smiled for the first time since reuniting. "I thought of it often enough, for I was very unhappy. I might have stayed in Melcombe and done better. Beyond all else, Oliver, I missed you. The things we did together. The talking. Laughing."

"It was the same for me, too," I said, and gave her an impulsive hug.

"I did contemplate a return to Melcombe, to you and Father, and accept my fate there. But by then I had almost no money. How was I to pay the fare for a return trip to Melcombe?

"I considered taking money from our uncle's shop, money I truly believed I was owed for wages. But I knew such an action would be wrong, and did not do so."

"That was wise," I murmured, thinking on what I had done.

"The one pleasure I derived came from the other young ladies who also worked in shops and stores upon Hanover Street. When we could find time, these young women and I would chat and gossip, sharing our sense of drudgery and misfortune."

I nodded and said, "Father once told me that 'Nothing in the world is more generously shared than unhappiness.'"

"It was during this time," Charity went on, "that I met Miss Belinda Peters. She was—in my eyes—a most clever, delightful, and prettyish person. London born, she knew the great city as well as she knew her fine hands. Her father was in trade, the candle business, where she, as I, was expected to work. Like me, Miss Peters chafed at restrictions.

"Miss Peters was acquainted with many people and knew where to find the many pleasures in this great city. Being a little older than I, and having experience of

244

London, it was natural she became my mentor. She included me in her company when we stole out at night when business was done.

"Beyond all else she was sure the only way to get free of parental tyranny was to have a pliable husband. She had great skills in dallying so as to attract young men."

"And did you?" I said, finding it painful to think of my sister doing such a thing.

"That's how I met Mr. John Avitable. I am mortified to tell you about him, but for you to understand what has become of me, I must."

"Please," I said.

"Mr. Avitable was a watchmaker's apprentice and had but one year of his seven years before he became a journeyman. Once done, he intended to set up his own shop.

"I found him exceedingly handsome, lively, with great wit and an honorable, prosperous future. True, he never had much ready money—apprentices rarely do—but when I could find the time away from my relations we put together our small funds and had much pleasure.

"Growing ever fonder of Mr. Avitable, I fell in love with him, and was sure he held the same sentiment for me. Of course I told him of my life in Melcombe, of you and Father.

"At the urging of Miss Peters, I exaggerated our father's income, suggesting it was about a hundred pounds a year. I more than hinted—another of Miss Peters's suggestions—that Father would provide a good dowry to the man who would have me as his wife."

"But Father hates the idea of dowries," I said.

"I put that aside, because Miss Peters's advice proved correct: when Mr. Avitable heard me speak of Father's wealth he soon professed an abiding affection for me, and bid me to marry him."

"What did you say?"

"I accepted. For his part he said he would marry me as soon as his apprenticeship was over, when he would become independent. Then he urged me to write to Father and tell him of my desire to marry him, that Father needed only to state in writing the dowry he would provide to make things settled. Mr. Avitable suggested fifty pounds as a marriage settlement.

"Hoping that for once Father would be sensible, I did write him, informing him of my circumstance, and asked him to commit himself to the money."

At this point, Charity's narration was interrupted by the ringing of the bells of St. Clements. During this loud and rather long pause, I could only look upon my sister and realize it was not just her clothing that had aged, but her youthful face as well. I also grasped that the letter Charity wrote must have been that second letter Father received in Melcombe, the night of the storm. I had no doubt, when he learned that Charity wished to marry and requested a dowry, it was sufficient cause to set him off for London.

When the bells ceased their ringing, Charity resumed her story.

"Believing I would soon be married, and free of my aunt and uncle's tyranny, I bridled more at their ill-usage. The result was a great row with Mrs. Cuttlewaith, who accused me of laziness and stupidity. Pushed into anger, I informed her that I'd be leaving soon to be married.

"In greater fury, she accused me of being a deceitful, lazy slattern and even blamed me for thievery, which was utterly untrue. She went to her husband, our uncle, and demanded he dismiss me immediately. I was turned out."

"Where did you go?"

"I hurried to Mr. Avitable and told him what had happened, and urged that we be married immediately and establish a home."

"Did you marry?"

"To my great horror, Mr. Avitable refused, saying that the world did not allow him to marry for mere love. Unless he had a proper dowry in hand—"

"The settlement?"

Charity nodded. "'When your father tells you what your dowry is,' Mr. Avitable informed me, 'and it is sufficient, you may apply to me again.'"

"What an unworthy man!" I cried.

"Oliver, I fear it's the way marriages are arranged."

"But Father didn't answer your letter, did he?"

"If he did, I no longer was living with our uncle and aunt, so there was no way he could reach me."

"What did you do?"

"Brokenhearted and distressed, being without a home, having only a few coins, I took myself to Miss Peters and appealed to her for help. She would not take me in but told me of one Mrs. Fulton, a refined lady—so she claimed—who had sufficient independent means to have established a charitable home for young ladies in distress.

"Not knowing what else to do, I took myself to this Mrs. Fulton. As it turned out, I was again deceived. Though Mrs. Fulton did have a home for young ladies, she brazenly informed me that all these young ladies were employed as thieves, who used their charms to steal from men who took a fancy to them. She further informed me that her business was under the protection of Mr. Wild, and that if I did not work with her she would inform him about me, telling that vile man I stole without sharing my proceeds.

"Against my will, she dragged me to where this Mr. Wild did his business at the King's Head, where he enrolled me among his underlings, coldly informing me that anything I stole must be turned over to this Mrs. Fulton.

"When we left Mr. Wild, I, enraged, foolishly told Mrs. Fulton I didn't need her permission, or anyone's, to be a pickpocket. I could do so on my own. I did not truly mean it—I had no desire to become a thief, but spoke out of resentment. I took myself away immediately and tried to find honest employment.

"Alas, I quickly learned that a young lady with no connections, recommendations, or immediate family to speak for her cannot find honest work in London.

"I was now one of the London's uncountable impoverished and homeless young women.

"Using the tiny amount of money that remained to me, I found a mean place where I could at least sleep in some safety.

"Altogether desperate, I made up my mind that I would become a pickpocket on my own, and steal only enough to take passage back to Melcombe."

"Have you actually . . . picked pockets . . . besides mine?" I asked with distressed reluctance.

"Just a few," she admitted faintly. "Oliver, otherwise, I would have starved to death. But despite having done what is wrong, it has led me to you, and now I feel saved."

Though astonished by all Charity said, when she had finished her tale, I said, "Tell me what that Mrs. Fulton looked like."

"What difference does that make?"

"Just tell me."

"She's tall with a narrow face, a double chin, and presumes to look haughty upon the world."

"The color of her hair?"

"Black, I think."

"I fear that this Mrs. Fulton has already informed Mr. Wild that you are working as a pickpocket without his permission. I saw her with him."

Charity gasped. "Do you know what that means?"

I shook my head.

"Then we are both in Mr. Wild's book and he will pursue us to the ends of the earth. Oliver, you and I have been forced to become Mr. Wild's thieves. It's not just the law who will pursue us. The most notorious criminal in England is seeking us even now."

CHAPTER FORTY-EIGHT

In Which Charity and I Try to Make Our Way.

I was unable to speak.

Then she added, "It's Mr. Wild who makes things so dangerous. You said Captain Hawkes works for him. I have heard many stories of his methods: The captain, fearing Mr. Wild will turn against him because of your escape, will go to great efforts to find you."

Recalling Mr. Sandys and his fate, I knew she was right.

"What are we going to do?" I returned.

"I don't know," she admitted. "I'll need to plan something. For the moment you need to come with me. At least we can hide for a while. And think."

Even as the bells of St. Clements church began to ring again, I followed my sister—neither of us talking—until we came to a place called Feathers Court, fairly close to the river Thames. The narrow court was a dead-end alley leading from Drury Lane and walled in by ancient wooden buildings, some of which were scorched black and on the verge of collapse. Huge timbers were wedged between them so as to prop one another up.

Five stories tall, these buildings had the look of boxes piled carelessly one atop the other, the way an infant might stack wooden blocks. Roofs were steeply peaked and had lopsided brick chimneys. The lower floor of one was all boarded up and seemed impassable, but Charity moved two staves. That created an opening, just enough to allow us to pass through. Once inside, she put the wood back.

The little light that came through the cracks revealed a cluttered space, cold and damp, a floor of rough dirt, and everything smelling foul. I could see a three-legged table, some unmatched chairs, and along the walls, what looked to be shelves. After a moment I realized people were lying on them. It was a hovel for the destitute.

Charity, a finger to her lips by way of urging silence, beckoned me to the far corner, into a tiny enclosed area, perhaps once a coal bin.

"This is where I stay," said Charity, sitting down on top of a heap of straw.

"How did you ever find such a place?" I asked as I

looked about. There was a pathetic neatness about the spot, as if Charity had tried to assert her true character.

"It was all I could afford," she replied. "It costs a penny every two days."

I gazed at her through the shadowiness and sighed. When childhood is at its best, there is a time when all seems good, smooth, and secure. Particularly for the youngest—such as me—bad times are not even imagined. All will go well. And no one seems more powerful than one's elder brother or sister. They can do no wrong. But when such saints fall from grace and become mortal, it is as if the whole world shifts from good to ill.

Thus we sat in silent gloom.

It was Charity who said, "You told me Father came to London to keep me from marrying. If he is here, he might be able to help us get home."

"But one of the reasons I came to London was to warn him not to come home because Mr. Bartholomew wishes to have him transported to the colonies. Moreover, I know now that Mr. Bartholomew works for Mr. Wild, too, and is in London now."

"Have you any idea where Father is?"

I shook my head.

"Does he know you're here?"

"No."

"We need to find him. He may be our best hope."

"Father might have gone to Uncle Cuttlewaith's home to inquire about you," I said, though I will admit, I was not certain Father could help us.

"If he did," said Charity, "I had already gone and our uncle has no idea where I went."

"But if Father did seek you at Mr. Cuttlewaith's home, he could have left an address where he might be found in case they gained some information about you. That's where we should begin."

Charity thought a bit and then said, "Our uncle would turn me away without even speaking. But since they have no anger against you, you could visit. In fact, I think it would be wise to say you don't know where I am."

"I'm willing," I said.

"But don't forget that Captain Hawkes and his friends will be watching for you."

"Charity," I said, "it seems as if everything we might do contains some danger. But if we don't risk something we are doomed."

She had to agree.

CHAPTER FORTY-NINE

In Which I Go to My Uncle Cuttlewaith's Home.

It was late evening by the time we had decided that I would visit our uncle's house. I would have gone right away but Charity insisted it would be unwise to pass through dark streets.

"I'm afraid your jacket would mark you as someone of wealth. You'd be set upon."

"I have no money."

"The footpads would be pleased enough to take your jacket," she said. "Constables come by rarely and are often one with thieves. As for those with the Watch, who are supposed to protect citizens, you can't depend on them either. I assure you, when the city is dark it's given over to crime. The wealthy always have bodyguards."

That evening, then, we remained where we were, first talking about all that had happened in greater detail, renewing our mutual deep affection. Most naturally we recalled happier times and even laughed at fond memories. At last we fell asleep, staying close so as to be loving and warm. I was secure in knowing there was no one else in the whole world I loved as well, and that she loved me, too. As I went off to sleep, I vowed I'd never part from her again.

It was a cold and clammy morning. As we prepared to go out, Charity cautioned me to keep a careful eye out for our enemies. "Your Captain Hawkes and his friends will almost certainly be searching for you," she warned me yet again. "Since I have no idea what they look like, it's you who must keep the sharp eye."

"And Mr. Wild," I reminded her, "will be searching for you."

I heard her rueful sigh.

Thus my spirits were depressed as we made our way through the decrepit space where Charity was living. I was sure there were more people lying about than when I came the night before. Not that anyone spoke to us.

Outside, a mungy brown fog filled the air, making it hard to see beyond a few feet. What I could see of the broken buildings on either side of the narrow court way seemed on the verge of collapse. Underfoot, our way was crusted over with sheets of thin, weak ice, which, once broken, spewed sticky sludge. I saw someone lying still against a building and wasn't sure if he (or she) was alive or dead. My new jacket did not keep me very warm. That air bore a foul stench.

Fortunately—if it could be considered fortune—Charity knew the streets well enough to guide us through the concealing fog to a place called Tom King's Coffee House. It stood in a lane off Covent Garden. Even if I had had directions, I never would have found it, the streets being all of a crisscross and despite the early hour already clogged with laborers.

The coffee house was crowded, most people appearing to be heavy-lidded with too little sleep or too much drink. Not much talk either, but a knick-knocking of clinking glass and cup. Charity and I barely spoke as we breakfasted on a penny's worth of bread and coffee. I kept alert for Captain Hawkes and his friends but saw nothing to alarm me. In truth, no one seemed to care about us as we huddled close in a darkful corner.

Our breakfast quickly consumed, we sallied out to the yet more busy streets. The low fog had become congealed by a dismal gray rain, which I was glad for, since I assumed it made us that much more difficult to see. Even so, not a person loomed before me that I did not scrutinize. Fortunately, no one gave me cause for alarm.

My uncle's house was on Hanover Street, not very far from Long Acre, near Covent Garden. It seemed a well-toned neighborhood, suggesting modest wealth. Streets were relatively clean, smelled better, and had fewer people about, and those appeared to be of higher quality.

From a distance Charity pointed to our uncle's store, one of a number of row shops. They were in brick buildings with street-level bow-front windows with displays of goods behind glass. Higher up were, I guessed, tenements where people lived.

My uncle's shop had a sign over the door that displayed a walking stick, painted gold. From the stick hung a sign that I could only just read:

SOLD AND REPAIRED
Walking Sticks for Fine Gentlemen
Mr. T. Cuttlewaith, Esq.

More importantly, I noticed some light moving behind the front window. "I think someone is about," I said.

"Business commences early and our uncle wants to lose none of it," said Charity. "He must be expecting a customer."

I found myself uneasy. "How do you think he'll treat me?" I asked, not really having considered the question before.

"It's only information you need. Just go," she said with

some urgency matched by a little shove. "You'll want to get in before anyone else does so you can speak freely. I'll wait for you here."

She retreated into an open alcove that kept her from the drizzle, but which allowed her to keep a watch on our uncle's shop.

I glanced at her for some final reassurance and then stepped away.

We all have relatives, and for some of us they are as numerous as they are close. But having been born and raised solely in Melcombe Regis, I had never met any of my kin, neither on my father's side nor on my mother's, not so much as a cousin. May I further remind you that my poor mother, having died when giving birth to me, was someone I had never seen. Nor had my father, in his everlasting sorrow, kept any images of her about our home.

Yet, as you might guess, an unknown parent brings to a bereaved child a thousand fanciful conjectures. You will understand then that I was most curious to meet this uncle of mine, seeking to gain, if you will, not just information about my father, but some sense of my mother.

I therefore approached the door with an odd mix of apprehension and expectation, pausing only to glance back to make sure Charity was still where she had retreated. Reassured, I drew breath and knocked on the door. After a few moments it opened.

CHAPTER FIFTY

In Which an Unexpected Meeting Takes Place.

It was a middle-aged man who opened the door and peered out. Despite the early hour, he was wearing a dark green gentleman's jacket, with wide sleeves, lace, and many buttons. Beneath a freshly powered wig his face was round, pink, with smooth cheeks. I could smell his orange-flower fragrance, so I supposed he was wishing to make an impression on someone. Since I was obviously not the person he was expecting, he considered me with a face shaped by displeasure.

"Yes?" he demanded.

For a moment I said nothing, merely stared at him as if I might somehow recognize my mother. Alas, I was met with instant disenchantment for this man appeared to my eyes as both dullish and ordinary. And no mother is ever ordinary to a child.

"Do you wish something?" he said when I did not reply speedily enough. There was spurning in his voice.

Recalling myself, I put on my cheerful smile and said, "Please, sir, are you Mr. Tobias Cuttlewaith?"

His look took on greater annoyance. "And if I was?" he returned.

"My name is Oliver Cromwell Pitts, sir. I believe you are my mother's brother. That, sir, would make you my esteemed uncle."

Upon hearing this intelligence, his face squinched up as if he'd just sucked on a sour lemon. "And if I were your uncle?" he asked.

"Please, sir, I've only just come to London. From Melcombe Regis. I'm trying to find my sister and father."

My words brought him even more animated aversion.

"Sir," I pressed, "I ask nothing from you, save that you might know of their whereabouts."

As it happened, some people were passing by on the street before his shop. They were of no particular account, but my uncle pulled the door open with some urgency. It was as if he did not wish to be observed with me.

"Come in," he said. "Just for a moment. I have an appointment with an important customer and I have no desire to be associated with your family."

I stepped forward.

It was a small shop, with a candle lantern sitting atop

a long table. Behind the table were panels upon which were affixed a great variety of canes and walking sticks, simple to elegant. On the table were some tools. On the walls were prints, which portrayed gentlemen in elegant dress—all with walking sticks.

When I entered, my uncle retreated, his back to his table, as if loath to be near me, hands clasped so as to suggest piety. He was staring at me intently.

"You look a bit like your mother," he said, his tone somewhat softened.

"Thank you, sir. I wish I had known her. But it's my sister who—"

A woman stepped into the room from a side way. I thought she must have been our uncle's wife and had been listening because in a curt, harsh voice she immediately said, "Your sister proved to be ungrateful and ill-mannered. We had to dismiss her. We have no idea where she went nor do we care."

"Yes, madam," I said, having no desire to argue. "But . . . my father? Might he have come here? He, too, was looking for her."

"Mr. Cuttlewaith," said my aunt, "tell this boy to depart."

Instead, my uncle considered me for a long moment. Perhaps by accepting me as his sister's son, he felt some obligation. "Your father," he said, "did come."

"And most unpleasant he was," inserted my aunt.

My uncle said, "I told him exactly what my wife told you—that I had to dismiss Charity and have no idea where she went. Your father strode away in a great anger, informing me that 'the law is king,' at least three times."

"Yes, sir," I said. "That sounds like him. But, sir, might he have possibly mentioned where he was lodging?"

"He requested—or should I say demanded—that if I received word of her, I should send the information to him at the Flying Horse Inn. That he would be staying there for a few days in hopes he might locate her."

"Could you share the location of that place with me, sir?"

"Turnstile Alley near Castle Street."

"Thank you, sir."

For a moment we just stood there, none of us knowing what to say, when we were interrupted by a knock on the door.

"The customer we're expecting," said my aunt. "I must ask you to go."

"Yes, madam," I said, content with the information I had received.

My uncle went by me and opened the door to Mr. Bartholomew's manservant.

CHAPTER FIFTY-ONE

In Which My Sister and I Seek My Father.

In this man's hands was Mr. Bartholomew's broken walking stick—you will recall it was damaged during the time his coach was waylaid. No doubt the servant was bringing the stick for repairs.

My uncle bowed him into his store.

The moment I recognized him, I knew I must get away. In haste I averted my face, hoping I looked somewhat different in the clothing Captain Hawkes had provided me. I burst past him and was instantly upon the street, heading for where Charity had been waiting.

I had barely gone ten steps when, from behind me, I heard, "Stop! Thief! Footpad! Stop him!"

The manservant, belatedly having realized who I was, was giving the hue and cry.

I raced to the spot where I had left Charity. She was not there.

Confounded, I stood desperately looking all about. The next moment Charity burst from another place and grabbed my arm. "I saw that person going into the shop, and feared there would be trouble and hid," she explained in haste. She was pulling at my arm and leading me away, both of us instantly speeding for all our worth.

"Who was that person?" she asked, moving quickly.

"Mr. Bartholomew's servant," I gasped. "He was the postilion on the stagecoach I was made to stop."

"Did he recognize you?"

"I fear so."

Charity made no response. But I knew her thoughts as if they were mine. It was as she had predicted. Our enemies were everywhere.

As we ran I stole a look over my shoulder. The foggy drizzle was still sufficiently dense that it was impossible to tell if the servant was following. In any case, there were already too many people on the street to distinguish anyone.

"Did you learn anything about Father?" asked Charity.

"Our uncle said he was at the Flying Horse Inn."

Charity immediately swerved into another direction. "This way," she said.

After a while I asked, "Are there no straight ways in London?"

"I'm going in a roundabout way in case we're being followed." She increased our pace.

CHAPTER FIFTY-TWO

In Which We Arrive at the Flying Horse Inn.

Turnstile Alley was yet another narrow way, leading from the much wider Castle Street to the major thoroughfare of Drury Lane. The Flying Horse Inn was midway in the alley, announcing itself by a small sign that depicted a white-winged horse. In the swirling, drizzly fog it seemed to be flying through the clouds. Oh, how I wished I had such wings that I, too, might escape.

The inn was an old, narrow building of two levels, its outside timbered, the spaces between the timbers filled in with I knew not what. There was one large door studded with big-headed nails.

Needing to catch our breath, we halted and gazed at the door, as if it might give us some clue to whether Father was within or not. I was trembling with damp, cold, and worry, continually looking up and down the street in fear that we had been tracked. If that was not enough, now that we were where Father might be, I found myself pulled in different emotional directions.

Yes, I wanted to find him, in hopes he would make our situation easier. Charity was right: he was a lawyer and that should prove helpful. And I needed to warn him about Mr. Bartholomew.

But as I knew only too well, he was a difficult man, given to doing things his own way, and poorly at that. Among the things he did poorly was being a parent.

My fear was that he might make things worse for us, not better. Perhaps before Charity had become a pursued thief, he might have helped. But now, with two of his children in jeopardy, plus Mr. Bartholomew's accusation to answer for, I feared all of us could be undone.

Though he had told my uncle he would be searching for Charity, it would not surprise me if he had not done so.

Having been thusly so often disappointed by him, I decided it would be better to leave the city immediately. The best way to secure our safety was by our own efforts.

It has oft been recorded that a parent can be embarrassed by an unruly child, and 'tis true, adults write manuals and tracts as to how best to treat such disobedient children. But it is all too often forgotten that there are times when a child is embarrassed by a wayward father or mother. A book of instruction—*How to Deal with Inept Parents*—might make a handy volume for many a youth.

I recalled my father's motto: "People care nothing for suffering. To get on you must mask your heart with false smiles." I think only then did I realize that was precisely the way I lived with him.

"Charity," I blurted out. "I think we should leave London right away. It's too dangerous to stay."

"I agree," she said, but even as she did, she knocked on the door.

After a few moments, when no answer came, I turned away hoping Charity would follow. Instead, she pulled me back while pushing the door open. I had little choice but to look inside.

It was a thoroughly gloomy place, with but two candle stubs barely burning. From what I could see, the room had just five tables, with chairs about.

At first it appeared as if no one was there. Then I heard the sound of snoring.

The person snoring was at first hard to see because the man was slumped over one of the tables, head resting on the wooden surface, hands dangling limply by his side. Atop his head was a lopsided wig. Before him were three bottles. I assumed they were empty.

Although the man's back was toward us, it hardly mattered. My heart sank. It was all that I had feared. By sound, sight, and circumstance, I recognized who it was. Many a time at the Golden Lion Inn in Melcombe Regis I had seen Father in this exact same posture. And so it was.

On the table before him was a backgammon board. No doubt he had been playing and gambling. I found myself wondering if he had won or lost.

In Melcombe, when my sister and I discovered Father in this fashion—drowned in his cups—we would manage to walk him back to our home on Church Passage. That was the end of it, until the next time. But here . . .

My sister and I exchanged knowing looks, the knowing full of despair.

Though I held back, Charity approached Father. She bent over him and into his ear whispered, "Father."

He stirred, slightly. "Father," she repeated more loudly. "It's me, Charity. And Oliver."

Father roused himself and sat up, albeit awkwardly, swaying as if sitting in a wave-tossed boat.

"Is it time to go . . . home?" he managed to say, only to droop over so that his head banged on the table. His snoring recommenced.

How can I express my sense of helplessness when

presented with this state of affairs? Consider: Have you ever seen a marionette, the kind of puppet held erect by strings in the hands of a person above? Think of me as such a puppet—and see what happens when the parental strings are cut. Collapsed. At that moment, that was me.

CHAPTER FIFTY-THREE

In Which We Seek to Find a Future

My sister sighed. "He doesn't even know where he is," she said.

"Or that we are here," I said, feeling betrayed. "He never did look for you," I added.

"Father," Charity said into his ear, "are you lodging here?"

He lifted a dirty, wobbly hand and with one finger extended, pointed toward the ceiling.

I looked up and around and noticed that far in the back of the room were steps leading up. Even as I saw them, I saw a man descending.

He was a short, stocky fellow with clumpy wooden shoes on his feet and a besmeared white apron tied round his waist. He barely reached the last step when, seeing Charity and me, he called out, "Who are you?"

"Please, sir," said Charity, "we are this man's children."

"Are you now?" He sounded unimpressed.

"His name is Mr. Gabriel Pitts. From Melcombe Regis."

"Aye," said the man. "That's him. He's been sitting there for a few days, he has. Playing backgammon. Won a ripe score, he has."

"Did he take a room here?" asked Charity.

"One floor up. Immediately to the right. Not that he's used it much. He's done nothing but play backgammon."

"Can we bring him up there?" Charity asked.

The man gave an indifferent shrug. "He's paid for it," he said. "You can always pay more."

Somehow we managed to bring Father to his room. It required all of us, my sister, me, and the innkeeper. We pulled, pushed, shoved, and prodded Father up the fifteen steep steps, he more sack of sea-coals than man. I am not even certain he knew what was happening.

Regardless, we got him into his room. It contained little more than a bed, a small table upon which sat a washing bowl and a candlestick. On the floor was a chamber pot.

We flung Father onto the bed, wherein he rolled over and continued sleeping. As he turned, many shillings, guineas, and even sovereigns poured from his pockets.

I knew my father gambled a lot, often winning. Let it also be clear that I felt gambling was sinful. But given our predicament, I presumed his winnings might mean he could yet take care of us, which I thought was good. Yes, it troubled me that something I thought bad might bring good, but I was beyond weary and unable to resolve yet another conundrum.

"Please, sir," said my sister to the tavern owner who had remained to look on. "May we stay with him?" Even as she spoke she handed him a coin from Father's hoard.

The man made no objections but put a finger to his brow and left, shutting the door behind him.

For a moment Charity and I stood and looked down at Father. His breathing was bubbly with spit and caused that small room to reek with his besotted breath. The sound of his snoring was like a grunting pig.

Feeling disgust, I said, "We should leave him."

"I can't quit him like this," said Charity, living up to her name.

I was prepared to go against the world, but not her.

Could we have truly left him then and there? I suppose so. Then why did we not go? Because whereas it is common belief that it is the parent who will not abandon a child, my experience is that it's the child who is far more reluctant to leave the parent. Surely Charity acted so. My emotions were equally conflicting: I felt the urge to give him one more chance even as I was telling myself he would be sure to disappoint. The world would have it that childhood is a sweet and easy time. The truth is, to be a child is hard.

During the next few hours, Charity and I remained in that small, stifling room. A solitary candle provided a pale yellow flickering, which threw out more dejection than light, the very replication of our minds.

As time wore on we used some of Father's money to purchase food from the tavern keeper. And Charity, in her fashion, endeavored to tidy the room, though there was little enough to adjust.

After perhaps two hours, I said, "He might sleep all day. I really think we should go."

"And not say good-bye?"

"He'll only swear to do better," I reminded her.

"I know," Charity acknowledged. "But I promise we shall leave as soon as he wakes."

Thus we waited. For the most part we used the time to talk about places to go. And though I must not foretell the future, suffice to say the place in fact we did go was nothing like we ever could have imagined.

CHAPTER FIFTY-FOUR

Reveals What Happened When Father Woke Plus a Shocking Turn of Events.

It took a while for Father to awaken. Upon partially opening his eyes and seeing Charity, the first thing he said was, "Did you marry?"

"No, sir."

"Then I have saved you," he muttered, closed his eyes again, and resumed his sottish snoring.

I turned to Charity. "Now can we go?"

"Soon," Charity whispered, though I thought she was about to cry. I sat down in a corner, pulled up my knees, and gave myself over to more frustrated waiting.

After some further time Father truly awoke. He did not seem to consider how odd it was that Charity and I were with him. But as I have said before, we had taken care of him many a time in his similarly swilled situations.

This time, however, he sat there, limp and looking forlorn, his wig off, revealing a head with a rough stubble of gray hair. His chin was grizzled, his eyes bloodshot, his lips slack, his ears tufted with gray hair, his neck skin wrinkled and flabby, prickled with white hairs, a ragged, untied neckcloth, a torn and dirty jacket. I was shocked by how tottery and decayed he appeared. I had never thought him old. I did so then. I found myself feeling sorry for him.

"What is this place?" he asked, making a general gesture of the room.

Charity told him.

"In what city?"

"London."

"London?" he slurred. "How long have I been here?"

"I'm not certain, sir," she said.

"And you," he said to me, "how did you get here?"

"It's a lengthy story."

"I will hear it," he said.

We told him our stories, Charity first, then I. He listened, head bowed. By turns he was angry, indignant, muttering now and again about a lack of justice. "Why did you accept such treatment?" he asked of us both.

"We didn't know what else to do," said Charity.

To me he said, "At least I arranged to provide you with sufficient funds."

"You did?" I said, taken by surprise.

277

"Of course!" he said with anger. "I left you a letter."

Angry, I yanked the smeared, crumpled letter from my pocket and thrust it at him. "This is what I found."

He gazed at it for a few moments and then began to read as if the smeared ink had melted away:

Oliver,

I received a letter which informed me that Charity is about to be married!! This is terrible news. I intend to stop it. I leave for London immediately. I will leave money for you with Mr. Webber at the Golden Lion where I take the stage. You can apply to him for such funds as you need.

I shall return when I can.
Your father,
Gabriel Pitts

"But I could not read it," I cried, thinking how altogether different things would have been if only I had done so.

"Then you believed I abandoned you!" he said with indignation.

"I hardly knew what to think," was my evasive answer. Fearing I may have misjudged him, I felt a jolt of self-blame.

I told him Mr. Bartholomew wished to lay a charge against him.

"I care that about the man," Father said and snapped his fingers. "I assure you," he added with majestic irrelevance, "the law is king." He turned to Charity. "But you did not marry."

"No, sir."

"Then all is well!" making it clear he did not understand our predicament. "Very good, then. We shall return to our Melcombe home," he announced. "Your suffering is over. I have won a great deal of money. All shall be good as it was."

In my state of confusion as to what I felt about Father, I looked to Charity. She drew herself up and said, "But Father, it was not good before. The truth is, you did abandon us long ago." Then she said, "You cared little for our suffering. To get on we did as you bid: masked our hearts with false smiles."

Charity's remark struck him hard. Deep. His body slumped more. His look turned bleak. Perhaps, too, the words went deeper, pushed further in by our hard expressions. He seemed to gain some understanding. Tears trickled down his dirty cheeks.

After a deep sigh, he said, "You are right. I have not . . . been a good parent. I promise to do better."

Alas, those words were only what Charity and I had heard Father say on many occasions. This time Charity said, "Father, I understand you mean well, but you must know that Oliver and I have decided that we can't go back to—"

She never finished the sentence because the door burst open. In stepped Mr. Bartholomew's manservant. He pointed right to me and cried, "There he is! The highwayman!"

Crowding in behind him was Mr. Bartholomew himself and Captain Hawkes, plus a man dressed in a blue cloth gown, whom I had never seen before. That man pushed to the forefront and proclaimed, "My name is Sergeant Constable John Roque, for the City of London. We arrest you in the name of the King's Majesty and we charge you to obey us."

As he spoke, he pointed in turn to my sister, my father, and me. My instantaneous thought was: we are all going to be hanged.

CHAPTER FIFTY-FIVE

In Which I Learn about the Wood Street Compter.

I'm not exactly sure how we managed to walk down the steps, but down we surely came, pushed and pummeled, all but falling, forced by those who came to arrest us. Outside there was a swirling cold gray mist, heavy, dank, and drab, which seemed brewed for the occasion.

On the street, strangers stopped to watch, some even hooting with derision. The only private words I heard were those spoken into my ear by Captain Hawkes, who, while holding me painfully by the neck, hissed into my ear, "You should have not deceived me. You had a great future and I had grown fond of you."

He offered no smile and I made no reply, though my thought was, Who deceived who?

As for Mr. Bartholomew, he was bleating words such as, "Now we shall see three rogues pay for their vile crimes!"

For his part, Father made a variety of loud, legal pronouncements, accusing the sergeant and the others of illegalities, a blatant ignorance of English justice. None of his words or arguments were answered. I doubt they were even considered. Of course, Father was in a state of considerable dishevelment, so that he hardly looked like an authority on anything. But he had both hands in his side pockets, which at least told me he had the wits to hold on to his money.

We were taken away, Sergeant Constable John Roque in the lead, the three other men—Hawkes, Mr. Bartholomew, and his servant—collaring each of us. Though Charity and I did manage to walk side by side behind Father, we said nothing. Our closeness did give some needful comfort, but I think we were in shock. As for where we were going, I didn't know, save that I'd heard the constable say, "We must proceed directly to the Compter."

As I would learn, the Compter was where prisoners were taken before a trial, the actual trials being held at the Old Bailey, at the court known as the King's Bench. This is to say, we were being swallowed by the legal system.

Fronting Wood Street, the Compter was a long, four-story brick building and an altogether dreary-looking place. Across the top three levels of the building were eight windows, all closed off by shutters. The lowest level had more windows, but they had bars as well as shutters. Clearly, this was not a building that welcomed light in any sense of the word.

Before the Compter's front door a variety of people had crowded wanting to get in, many carrying odd parcels— food and blankets—to those already confined. As we approached, they were forcibly shoved aside and could make no defense save abusive words.

We three were hurried forward into a shabby vestibule, at the head of which was a desk. Sitting behind it was a man who immediately reminded me of nothing so much as a skeleton.

He wore no wig, which made his hairless head quite skull-like. His face had hollow cheeks, a small stub of a nose, a receding chin, and hollow, dark rimmed eyes. His eyebrows were but faint, and his slack mouth revealed a row of teeth like a broken fence. For clothing, he wore a filthy brown robe with great wide sleeves, from which dangled long fingers with yellowing fingernails.

On the table before this disagreeable-looking man was a large book of many pages, already spread wide, like a gaping mouth. To one side lay a quill pen and a stubby bottle of ink. To his other side was a small wooden box.

Behind this man, lounging on a bench, were two rough-looking and burly men.

The sergeant constable marched us right up to the skinny man. "Prisoners, sir!" he called. "All three of them. A vicious gang."

The man looked at us with his big eyes and spoke to Father, "Sir, I am Mr. Witherington, the turnkey here. Be so good as to provide your names."

Before we could answer, Mr. Bartholomew shouted out—while pointing—"Mr. Gabriel Pitts, Master Oliver Pitts . . . I don't know the chit's name."

"Charity Pitts," said my sister.

"Can you write your names?" inquired Mr. Witherington.

"We can," said my father.

"Very good then, sir," said Mr. Witherington. "Write those names in the book here." Lifting up the quill pen he dipped it daintily into the inkpot and with a polite gesture offered it to my father. "And, please, you sir, pay your entry fee, the garnish. One shilling for each of you. If you don't have it, I'll be obliged to strip off your coats and shoes."

As he spoke the two men behind him stood up, making it clear that they would be quite willing and able to take our garments if requested.

"Such fees are extortion and illegal," pronounced my father. "And I am a lawyer."

Mr. Witherington gestured to the men behind him, and in a rather mild voice said, "Sir, I appreciate the fact that you have your profession. I have mine. These men are all the legality I need, sir. Now, sir, pay in cash or coats."

Father, with contempt, threw three shillings on the table. Unperturbed, the turnkey scooped them up and flung them into his box as if they were pebbles.

"Now, sir," he said, "be so good as to inscribe my book."

The three of us wrote down our names. My hand was shaky.

"Very well," continued the turnkey, "I am pleased, sir, to offer you a choice of accommodations. The weekly rates are the master's side, ten shillings, six pence. The knight's ward, five shillings, or the hole, three shillings. Or," he added with a visible sense of disgust, "you may sleep over the cellar drain or sit up with other prisoners who are not as blessed as you. You may be sure, sir, it matters nothing to me. Still, my professional advice, sir, which I offer free of fee, is that if you are going to be hanged—and I presume you will be hanged—you might, as I often say, provide yourself with a dab of delight before you dangle." He grinned hideously at his own jest.

Father asked, "When is our trial?"

"When I tell you it is to be held, sir," was the answer.

At that point my father said, "The sooner it takes place, the more money I shall give you." Quite plainly and openly, he was offering a bribe.

"Admirable!" cried the turnkey with another appalling grin. "Well said. I appreciate a gentleman of keen understanding. We shall get on well, sir. We shall. I do believe money is the language of universal understanding. Now, sir, I pray you, what room do you desire?"

"We shall take the master's side," said my father.

"Excellent, sir. Of course there is also a fee for my assistants that they might have a bucket of drink."

Another payment.

"And you may fee them, sir, to guide you to your accommodations. You don't wish to go into the wrong room, sir. No, sir, you most decidedly do not."

Another payment.

"Very good, sir. You will be informed as to the costs of food, fuel, and water," said the turnkey, adding, "Number nine!" at which point the men behind him beckoned us to follow.

"I shall see you in court," cried Mr. Bartholomew after us. "Just know that I intend to stand witness against you, as will Mr. Jonathan Wild, among other witnesses. The law is king!" he bellowed.

At those words Mr. Witherington held Father back. "It might please you to know, sir, that the great Mr. Wild himself was once accommodated in this very place. He, too, was a gentleman of keen understanding. And he appreciated us, sir, and by way of proof, sends many a culprit this way."

Dazed, I followed along as the turnkey's assistants led us deep within the Compter, down a long, dim corridor, upon whose wall I could see a series of closed doors.

A door was thrown upon. "Here you are," said one of the men.

As we stepped into the room, my father placed a coin in each of the men's hands. "Some sea-coal for heat," he said.

"Yes, sir."

The door slammed. A lock snapped loudly. We were in prison.

CHAPTER FIFTY-SIX

In Which I Describe What Happened to Us.

The cell was small and fusty, smelling of having been populated by too many putrid people too many times. It had no window. There was a little table, a rickety chair, a low, narrow bed, with a piece of ragged cloth for a mattress. No blankets. The floor was filthy. The hearth empty. A washbasin and chamber pot had been provided, lacking only water. On the wall hung a badly printed image of King George, who for all the world looked (perhaps on purpose) like a bewigged and pout-mouthed frog. Such was the Compter's best accommodation.

When we came in, Father instantly threw himself upon the bed, such as it was, and just lay there, his dirty wig tipped forward, partly covering his eyes. It was hard to know if he was exhausted, appalled, or simply unwilling to acknowledge the world in which he found himself. I rather feared all three.

Charity and I stared at each other, until I went forward and hugged her and she hugged me. It was the only comfort available. Truly, in the whole world she was my greatest ease. I hoped I was the same for her. While nothing was said, we had no expectations that Father could help us.

A short time later the door was unlocked and one of the men brought in some sea-coal, which he dumped into the hearth, lit it, and started to leave.

My father called out: "I require a small leather sack!"

"It will cost," said the man.

"Of course." Father didn't even ask the price.

The room, being small, quickly warmed; a luxury in our bone-chilled state.

Charity went by the side of the bed and said, "Father, what is going to happen to us?"

With effort, he sat up and rubbed his dirty face with an equally dirty hand. "To repeat myself: know that I shall not abandon you. You are my children," he went on, "the issue of my late wife. I have but little love left within me, but such as I have is entirely yours. Let me acknowledge that I realize I have this one last chance to be of use to you." Grandly, he put a hand over his heart. "I shall not fail you."

"You have said as much before," Charity said.

"True. All too true. But if I fail you this time, we shall hang. In other words, this will be my last opportunity to be a responsible parent.

"Now then, the better to defend you, I need to hear all your so-called crimes."

"We told you," I said.

"I wasn't listening."

But before either of us could speak, Father added, "Be forthright. Skip explanation as to how or why you committed your crimes, even if you did not commit them. It's only accusations that matter here. Charity, you first."

She stood mute, and I know, ashamed.

"Reveal all," commanded Father. "I give you my word; I'll not judge you, but endeavor only to help you."

Oh, how much I wanted to believe him!

With effort Charity said, "Before I left Melcombe, I took some shillings from your money-box, enough to pay for the coach to London, but when you gave me sufficient funds, I returned it."

Father, true to his word, showed no emotion, but only said, "I thought as much. Go on."

"Here, in London, when impoverished, I picked a few pockets."

"A few. Humph. Very well, what did you take?"

"Handkerchiefs."

"Silk, linen? Cotton?"

"Some silk, some linen."

"What did you do with them?"

"Sold them in a shop."

"For what money?"

"Thirteen shillings for silk. Two for the linen."

"Very well; if you are found guilty, according to the current law, which is cheerfully known as 'The Bloody Codes,' your crimes mean you could be hanged, transported to the colonies, branded, placed in a pillory, or whipped. The pillory often means death by the street mob. And if you return from transportation before your time that, too, would be a hanging offence."

"You are harsh, sir!" I cried.

"Master Oliver," he said, "if I have learned any truth in my life, it is that truth is almost never soft."

Charity lowered her head and began to cry. I put my arm around her. As for Father's remark, I made no reply.

"Or," said my father—but not with much power—"you could be acquitted."

He turned to me. "Now then, Oliver, what are your unspeakable crimes?"

"I took twenty-three shillings from a dead wreck on the beach at Melcombe. But I did not take all I could have taken. Just enough for food. Then Mr. Bartholomew discovered I had taken it."

To which my father blithely replied, "A hanging offence."

"I was forced to help rob a stagecoach."

"Being forced will have nothing to do with it. Another hanging offence. Anything else?"

I repeated what I had already told him regarding Mr. Probert at the Melcombe poorhouse.

"You are lucky there. Most likely merely a whipping offence. Or perhaps a hand branding. I am impressed, Oliver: In a short time you have acquired a varied list of offences. Anything else?"

I said, "I was kidnapped."

"Just know that according to English law, kidnapping is not a crime."

My sister looked at Father. "What will you be charged with?"

"Since Mr. Bartholomew is involved, I will be charged with cheating and that is considered theft. Which means, I, too, must hang. But upon my honor, I do not cheat when I play backgammon. I am an excellent player. Mr. Bartholomew, of course, will testify otherwise. But then he is a fool. There is an old English saying: 'A fool and his money are soon parted.' One might say as much for heads.

"Happily, in these past few days I won a great deal. Such funds will be as useful as they are necessary. I have often said, 'The law is king.' Given our current circumstance, I am willing to acknowledge a more painful truth: as the turnkey might have said, 'Money is king.'

"Now then," he continued, "any one of us may go free. Or, all three of us could hang. It may give pleasure to know that if we do hang, we will probably be hanged together—as a family. It should provide a singular entertainment for the London crowd. And we shall, hopefully, enter Heaven linked."

I said, "Is there nothing we can do?"

To which my father replied, "I shall have to think. To be detained in London's prisons is in itself a kind of death. My first hope is that we shall have a speedy trial. I already said I would pay for that. But in life," he added, "we must expect the unexpected."

With that he lay back down, pulled his wig over his eyes, and appeared to become lost in thought.

We were in the Wood Street Compter for three days. It might have been very much longer, but Father's money made a difference. Still, it would be meaningless to describe what happened there, because nothing happened. Save one thing over and over again: everything, heat, water, food (corrupt as it was), emptying the chamber pot, candles, all had a cost. Money was demanded for everything. Father paid. We were fortunate that he could. After all my harsh thoughts regarding him I was grateful.

The early morning of the fourth day, there was a loud

knock on the door. It was the turnkey. "We must shackle you," he announced. "Your trial is today."

Even then, in order to leave the Compter we had to pay a seven-shilling fee each, and another three shillings to the turnkey.

In England one had to pay even to be hanged. And it was expensive.

CHAPTER FIFTY-SEVEN

In Which My Father, Sister, and I Are Brought to the Court.

That morning proved yet another cold, gray day, but fortunately no rain or fog. Father—clinging to his bulging leather bag—Charity, and I were lined up among some fifty or so prisoners, men, women, and children. A few men were fashionably dressed. Most were not. Many were in rags. Some tried to make a joke of the moment, but most were singularly somber. Most of the children were crying.

A long and heavy metal link chain was fixed around our right wrists, and then extended to the person behind. Some ten people came before Father. Then came Charity and I, followed by all the rest. I clung to a vague hope that Father would do something, but I had no reason to believe he could.

It was Mr. Witherington the turnkey who led this wretched parade down the street named Old Bailey. As it happened, the courthouse building was two hundred yards or so northwest of St. Paul's Cathedral, of which I could see only its immense gray dome topped by a cross. I found it hard to appreciate its beauty.

Though I suppose I was a Nonconformist like Father, upon seeing the great church—the established Church of England—I quickly made a prayer. Alas, there was no angelic interceding, and we were led into the court itself.

To my surprise the courtroom was outside a large building, which is to say in the open air, in an unroofed yard. In a high recess of that building—on the ground floor—was a tall, long table behind which bigwigged judges sat, the high judge in the middle. They were covered by a kind of roof. To either side of that long desk was a place for members of the jury to sit. Below the desk, another long table, around which sat black-robed, white-wigged men. I had no idea what they did.

Standing in front of that high judge's desk was a railed enclosure, the so-called dock, where, as I would soon learn, the accused faced the judges. The only women in the court were prisoners.

The area inside the yard—the place where we prisoners stood—was enclosed by a high brick wall, topped by sharp-looking metal spikes. I suppose those spikes were there to keep us from escaping.

The chief judge was Sir Peter Delmen, a large, grossly fat-faced man, who embodied pomposity and power. He never smiled, but shaped his plump red lips into a perpetual scowl, lower lip extended, while he kept his eyes half lidded, suggesting that merely to see the prisoners was a rank offence to his eyes. His great white wig flowed down over his broad shoulders, as if Heaven's clouds had gathered round his head, and he peeked out at mere mortals. His robe was blood red, cut short at the sleeves, while extended white undersleeves reached his interlocked pink, puffy, and well-manicured hands.

To either side were other judges looking much the same. They put me in mind of a row of birds of prey sitting on a fence.

The trials soon got under way and to my mazement the individual judgments were hardly more than fifteen or twenty minutes in length for each accused person.

Charges were read. Witnesses, under oath, made statements. The accused was allowed to speak, but he (or she) had no lawyer to speak for them, not even the children. Rather, the prisoner was allowed to make a plea, which clearly was of pathetic use.

Next, juries were consulted. In haste they consulted

after which they shouted out their verdicts—mostly "Guilty!" Then the chief judge pronounced a sentence.

A man stole a horse. He was condemned to be hanged.

A boy cut down a tree in a garden; in his sobbing plea he claimed he was cold and only wanted to use the wood for heat. He was sentenced to seven years transportation.

Someone was accused of shoplifting a bolt of cotton cloth valued at five shillings. He, too, was to be transported. For fourteen years.

Another boy broke the window of a shop after five in the evening (the hour seemed to have some bearing in the charge) and that was a hanging offence. He was led off, shrieking horribly.

But then, it was all horrible. Endlessly ghastly and cruel judgments. Endless indifference to pleas and circumstance. Yes, real crimes were presented, but they were treated in no ways different than trivial acts.

What would be my sentence? I kept thinking. My increasingly frantic hopes turned toward marvels: that I might become invisible, or turn into a flea so I could hide in someone's wig, or perhaps miraculously become a flying horse. Useless wishes like that. Needless to say, I remained myself, my miserable self.

During that one long day—and it was truly terrible—among my fellow and sister prisoners, six were accused and found guilty, receiving sentences of death by hanging.

Forty-seven were found guilty and sentenced to be transported to the American colonies. Seven more were found guilty and were to be branded on the hand with a hot iron. Six others, also guilty, were to be whipped. One old man was fined and sent to suffer three months' imprisonment.

Only one person was acquitted.

Oh, wicked world where to be merely whipped is thought a kindness!

We three were included in my summation. This is what happened.

Exactly how many hours we were there, I don't know. I do know that the tension I felt at not knowing my fate was almost too much to bear. My stomach was a fist. My head a lump of lead. My heart weak with pounding. Though I felt like crying out for sympathy for all of us, I did not do so. I had no energy.

After a while, anything the court said to me would have been a relief. Just tell me my fate! I felt like shouting. Don't torture me so.

Of course I stayed mute. Enforced silence brings loud pain.

At some point in time, someone—I know not who—called out our names: "Mr. Gabriel Pitts, Master Oliver Pitts, and Mistress Charity Pitts."

Our trial was about to begin.

CHAPTER FIFTY-EIGHT

In Which We Come to Trial.

Staying close together, we were moved toward the prisoners' dock—and climbed the narrow, rickety steps to the little uneven platform, railed in on three sides. There we stood, my little family, midst a sea of faces, only some of which were looking at us with emotions ranging from indifference to hostility. Nary a friendly face did I see anywhere.

"Let me do the talking," Father whispered to us.

Below, various officials, black robed and bewigged, barely considered us. The jury men in various dress and most with wigs sat in slouching poses, some not even looking at us. One, I am sure, was asleep.

A black-robed man sitting below the judges stood up.

"Clerk of the court," Father whispered.

This clerk read the charges against us, and they were

fairly well what we had anticipated: My father cheating at backgammon. I was accused of stealing money from a wrecked ship, aiding and abetting a highway robbery, assaulting a children's poorhouse headmaster. My sister charged with being an aggravated pickpocket. Furthermore, the clerk said we were a family of wicked thieves, a veritable gang, which prompted a reign of misrule in the kingdom.

"How do you plead?" intoned the judge.

"Not guilty," cried Father.

"Let us hear from witnesses!" said the clerk.

It must be noted that each of the following witnesses swore an oath that they would tell nothing but the truth.

The first witness was Mr. Bartholomew, decked out in his finery like a man-o'-war dressed in bunting, who informed the court first of his importance. Then, pointing to me with his walking stick, he said, "This wicked boy caused a ship to be wrecked by building a fire on the Dorset coast, thereby luring it to shore. Ignoring the suffering and hurt sailors, he broke through the ship's hull and stole a tar's lifetime wages from his very bed of rest. From there he went on to become part of a vicious highway gang that stopped a stagecoach and stole Crown revenues. From me, my Lord, from me!"

Considering my age and size and strength, it was all monumentally absurd. When no one objected, it took all my willpower not to scream out, "Lie-teller! Rogue! Shake-bag!"

"But," Mr. Bartholomew continued, "it is no wonder the boy took to crime: His father is a notorious cheating gambler. My lord, if England is to be safe, you must make an example of father and son."

The next witness was none other than his manservant. Pointing to me, he said, "That boy brazenly halted a stagecoach so as to allow it to be robbed by a mob of masked men. He may look young, my lord, but he was the leader of this gang of highwaymen."

Then Captain Hawkes spoke. "My lords, I worked very hard to keep that boy"—he gestured to me in a courtly way—"from a life of crime, but against all my kind advice, he persisted in his thievery. My lords, I speak as a parish minister's son. May I add, sirs, that jacket he is even now wearing, I do solemnly swear, he stole from me."

Finally, Mr. Jonathan Wild came forward. When he did there was a stir in the crowd, as though some great luminary had burst into view. He was, as I had seen him before, scowling, but he was now shaved smooth. Dressed all in black—like a parson—his look was severe, as if he bore the burden of great judgment. His hat was in his hands but his coat was open, and as before, I could see that he still carried a pistol.

"My lords, as chief thief-taker general of Great Britain

and Ireland," proclaimed Mr. Wild, "it was I who arranged for the arrest of this notorious Melcombe Regis gang. May I call my lords' attention to the fact that this band includes the infamous pickpocket Charity Pitts, sadly misnamed, who has stolen countless silk handkerchiefs from many a gentleman."

To hear all these utterly untrue accusations left me nothing less than dumbfounded. They were preposterous. Beyond belief. Farcical fictions. I was reminded of my father's phrase, "A man should be known, not by his friends but by his enemies."

So we were.

But no one objected until the clerk asked Father if he had anything to say.

Father leaned out of the dock. "My lords," he shouted. "You have heard nothing but sheer nonsense! Skimble-skamble! Not one word of it is true. All perjury."

"Is that all you have to say?"

"I have spoken the truth, my lords. In this kingdom, surely that should be enough."

From somewhere I heard a snicker. I was astonished, utterly crushed that Father offered absolutely no further defense. His brief tirade seemed useless.

Next moment the chief judge—who had not previously spoken—turned to the jury and said, "Have you a verdict?"

The men in the jury huddled together for a few brief moments. Even the sleeping man was prodded awake. All too quickly one of the men stood up. "All guilty," he announced.

"Very well," said the judge to us. "You are all sentenced to be hanged."

CHAPTER FIFTY-NINE

In Which I Reveal What Happened Next.

❧❧❧

The sentence was given carelessly. No ceremony. No emotion. Just said. Hardly more than a mere "hallo" or "good-bye." Hearing those words was a piercing blow to my heart, causing deep and awful agony. I could not think or breathe, though I could weep, and did, the kind of choking, sobbing cry that shakes the whole body and soul. Charity wept, too. We stood there, heads bowed, trembling hands linked together. Who else had we to cling to?

The judge intoned, "Have you anything more to say?"

"Yes, my lord, I do," Father cried out, leaning out of the dock. "I do!" Then he did the most extraordinary thing: he held up that leather bag, the one he had purchased in the Compter and brought along. "My lord, may I approach the bench?"

The chief judge looked up and perhaps for the first

time I saw him smile. "You may do so," he said, quickly recovering a severe look.

Father, clutching the leather bag, hastily climbed down from the dock and fairly ran through the crowd of prisoners, until he reached the judge's desk. Standing as tall as he could, he plumped the bag heavily on that desk. It landed so heavily I could hear it clink.

The judge leaned forward. Words were exchanged. Father made his way back to the dock. I watched him come, and when I glanced over to the judge, I saw that the bag was gone.

Then the judge made an announcement: "An appeal for clemency has been asked and granted by the mercy of this court. Master Oliver Pitts shall not be hanged, but be transported to the American colonies for seven years. Mistress Charity Pitts, likewise not hanged but also to be transported to the same place for seven years. Mr. Gabriel Pitts, acquitted. Next case!"

It's hard to give a full expression to what I felt. A marvel to have gained an unexpected life; wonderful to have the hanging noose withdrawn, delightful to be Lazarus-like, breathing the London air, foul though it was.

The next moment that joy was jolted by a dreadful new realization: I had been banished from England. Thrown out. Much more than banished. Transportation meant that for seven years I was to be a slave somewhere in the American colonies. Whereas I thought I knew what death might bring with all its terrors, I knew absolutely nothing about living in those remote places, save they were across a vast and hazardous sea. What would become of me?

The only softening of this terrible exile was that I felt relief that Charity and I would remain together. For had not the judge said, "Mistress Charity Pitts, likewise not hanged but also to be transported to the same place for seven years."

Unexpected lives indeed.

But, lackaday, there was more to come.

CHAPTER SIXTY

In Which I Experience an Unexpected Ending.

B elieve me," Father whispered as we were led down from
the dock. "I tried to bribe the judge for all our lives."
He was pleading to us now, pleading with embarrassment.
"It was the judge's perversity that acquitted me," he added.
"I asked clemency for all. At least I saved your lives."

That certainly was true. I felt gratitude. But I felt bit-
terness, too. I did not think of myself as a criminal. I did
not think so of Charity either. As far as I could think it
through, we had been forced into crime. Yet here Charity
and I had been turned into slaves.

The verdict also served to further separate us from
Father. A pity that, for he had proved—in his fashion—
that he did care for us.

In a low voice he also said, "I have saved a little money."

With chains heavier than when we came to court, now

on wrists and feet, Charity and I were led from court. Father, acquitted, followed along as best he could. He was free. We were going to Newgate.

Newgate Prison is the ancient stone prison infamous for its filth, corruption, and deprivation. Earlier in my account, I quoted Mr. Daniel Defoe's (he who wrote *Robinson Crusoe*) sweet words about Melcombe. Regarding Newgate Prison, the same author wrote: "Such wickedness abounds that the place seems to have the aspect of Hell itself." He spoke true: the Compter, by comparison, was a graceful palace.

Along with other prisoners we were brought into the entryway, something called the lodge. Immediately a demand was made of two shillings, six pennies to remove our irons. Then we prisoners were further divided, women from men so that Charity and I were instantly separated.

More choices: the master side for those who could pay fees, the common side for those who could not. Those who could pay gave six shillings and sixpence to the turnkey, plus more to the steward, who was the longest surviving prisoner in the jail.

By paying more than twenty pounds, Father secured me (and I presumed for Charity) the best accommodation, which meant a small room with a wooden floor and one window. Crowded. Beyond that he had to pay for the most ordinary comforts, food and drink. If you did not pay you were stripped, beaten, and generally physically abused. The truth is, as at the Compter, there was nothing for which one did not pay. A fellow prisoner told me the prison warden had paid some five thousand pounds for the wardship of Newgate. It was clear he was determined to wring back his investment.

The air was bad. Filth was everywhere. When I walked about, there was a crunching sound, which, as I discovered, came from stepping upon the vast numbers of fleas and lice that lived on the floors.

It was not unusual for transported felons to wait long times—months—in Newgate before being shipped out. As a result many died there before their time. Mind! If you died in Newgate, your family was required to buy your corpse—if they wanted it.

Our great luck was this: we were sent off within a few days.

Though it happened much faster than normal, the common practice was this: We were purchased by some shipping agent for three pounds. He would carry us across the Atlantic Ocean, then once in America, he would sell our seven years' labor for ten pounds.

Our few days' imprisonment passed. Charity and I both remained protected by Father's open purse. He, like a repentant sinner, bestowed more care for us than we had ever experienced from him before.

On the day we were to board the oceangoing ships, just as when we had been marched from the Compter, a great crowd of prisoners was handcuffed two by two. These prisoners were mostly young men and women, plus children, for these were the people easiest to sell in America for labor.

Charity and I were bound together, as we wished it, and as Father paid for.

He also marched along with us. I shall be honest: we paid little attention to him.

As we passed through the London streets, there was much weeping and wailing among the prisoners, for people understood they were unlikely to see family ever again. If they outlived their transportation time, they might never come back.

Along the street many Londoners shouted abuse and wished us well out of country. Many a rotten vegetable and worse were flung at us. "Good riddance," was the general tone of their remarks and actions.

Being linked by iron, and love, Charity and I walked side by side. To go together in misery, I suppose, is to make less of that misery.

Father walked by our side. At one point I asked him where he would go.

To my surprise he said, "Once I have raised enough funds I intend to go to America and join you so we can be reunited. There can't be less justice than is here, and perhaps in the colonies there will be more."

"I pray so," Charity said.

We were led down to the edge of the Thames River, via the Blackfriars steps. We understood we'd be placed in small oar-driven boats, taken to the transatlantic ship, and then drop down the Thames and depart as soon as tide and wind proved favorable.

At the top of Blackfriars steps Father slipped some coins in our pockets, gave us final embraces, and said, "We shall meet again. Stay together."

It was only when we reached the bottom step that disaster came.

Just as we were about to walk into the little boats, the line of prisoners was divided.

I was forced into one boat.

Charity was forced into another.

"We can't be separated," I cried, resisting my guard's hand and trying to hold on to Charity. With a blow he simply knocked me down. "You go in different ships," he said.

"But where?" I cried in great anguish.

"Who cares," said the sailor.

If ever a heart was finally broken, surely mine was then and there. I sat in one small boat, Charity in another. The boats pulled away from shore and once upon the great river, they moved toward different ships.

I looked back. Father was standing on the steps, his face red with useless fury.

Swinging around I watched Charity's boat move farther away, oars working in unison, like some multi-legged water beast. Her frightened, weeping face was turned toward me, as mine was turned to her. I shouted out a sacred vow:

"I will find you, Charity! I promise!"

Charity opened her mouth and no doubt returned my call, but the words were lost in the splash of oars and the moans and wails of my fellow prisoners. Would I ever, I wondered, hear the voice of my beloved Charity again?

I turned toward London, gazed upon its multitude of buildings, its church spires, and its vast crowds of people—its monsterish being—and hastily closed my eyes. Then and there, even as I was being pulled away, I swore that I would never be a slave.

And more: In some way, in some fashion—no matter what or how long it took—I would restore our freedom.

[To be continued in Book Two]

A NOTE FROM THE AUTHOR

On pages 139 and 179 of his story, Oliver records the words of a song he overhears. In fact, the song he mentions comes from *The Beggar's Opera*, by John Gay, first performed in 1728, some four years after Oliver's story takes place. Gay's song so perfectly captures the spirit of the times, I could not resist including it. It probably didn't exist in 1724, but it certainly could have.

While the events and characters in this story are based on history, they are the product of my imagination, with one notable exception: Jonathan Wild was a real person, a most notorious and truly wicked man. In his lifetime, he was Great Britain's preeminent criminal, who stole vast sums by pretending he was on the side of the law. When it suited him, he betrayed those who worked for him and sent them to death or transportation. His exploits were written about often (including by Daniel Defoe and Henry Fielding), and he was the model for many a literary criminal mastermind, including, perhaps, Fagan in Charles Dickens's *Oliver Twist* and Moriarty, Sherlock Holmes's archenemy, as written by Arthur C. Doyle.

In May of 1725, Wild was in turn betrayed and then executed before a huge audience. His body was taken to the Royal College of Surgeons for dissection. If you are so inclined, you may view his skeleton in the Royal College's Hunterian Museum in Lincoln's Inn Fields, London.